I0571283

Triple Diamond

HEART OF THE STORM

GEMMA SNOW

Heart of the Storm
ISBN # 978-1-83943-806-6
©Copyright Gemma Snow 2019
Cover Art by Erin Dameron-Hill ©Copyright September 2019
Interior text design by Claire Siemaszkiewicz
Totally Bound Publishing

HEART OF THE STORM

Dedication

To all the readers who followed this series, I am
eternally grateful. Thank you for joining me on
another Triple Diamond adventure and for
everything.

Prologue

"Why can't Casey go?"

Hollie's voice was resolute and she did her best to keep the panic from rising further up her chest and into her throat, where it would inevitably clog her speech and undermine the powerful, capable persona she had been carefully crafting for nearly a decade.

"Casey isn't the Response Director for Region VIII, Callihan. You are." Debra Lewitt was a damn good boss to have for people who traded in emergencies, but Hollie really wished that the woman's icy exterior would melt just a little right now.

Which was a rather poor analogy, considering that Hollie wouldn't be in this situation if the Black Reef Mountain Range wasn't about to drop a historic amount of snow runoff into Lewis and Clark County.

"We need you in Montana by Sunday night at the latest." Lewitt dropped the folder onto Hollie's desk and folded her arms, giving Hollie the expression that she had clearly given hundreds of subordinates and superiors over the years. Hollie got it. Of course she did. Working in any government agency as a woman was challenging enough — she could only imagine how much more difficult it would be to find respect as a woman of color. But she wasn't being an asshole for asshole's sake, she just...

She was just terrified to go back.

The moon would have been better. Hell, Los Angeles or New York would have been a fine substitute, because they were farther away, and farther away was preferable because Hollie's cozy office in downtown Denver suddenly felt far, *far* too close to the mountains of Wolf Creek, Montana. And everything else she would find there.

Every*one* else.

"Callihan." Lewitt bent down over her desk. "Where's your head?" This was said with a modicum of emotion, which meant things had to be pretty bad. Hollie never had been very good at hiding what she felt.

"There's a lot of history for me in Wolf Creek, ma'am," Hollie managed. "I haven't been back to that town for nearly a decade."

Lewitt's features softened almost imperceptibly, but Hollie had been working at Debra Lewitt's side for nearly five years, and she had become an expert at reading the micro-emotions.

"Maybe it's the right time for you to take this trip," she said, giving Hollie a far too discerning gaze.

Or maybe even the idea of those old haunts makes you feel vulnerable.

Or maybe.

"I'm not so sure everyone there will agree." Hollie half-whispered, unsure whether she was speaking to her superior or to herself. It also wasn't necessarily true. She had no idea what the reception would be upon her arrival. Hell, they could have forgotten all about that night. All about her.

The idea that such a defining moment in her life could be so easily replaced with a white picket fence or two-point-three children didn't sit well with Hollie, but she had made her choices and she would make the same ones given the chance. She hadn't regretted her decision to leave in years.

Much.

"Then don't go to make friends," Lewitt replied. "We deal in emergencies every day, Callihan."

She took a deep breath and released it very slowly. "Hollie, look at me."

Hollie looked. They'd been in their fair share of shit-show situations together, on the ground and in the 'war room', as they affectionately called working in disaster and emergency relief for one of the snowiest, wettest, driest and most-tornado-y regions in the country. That sort of life-or-death environment could really bring people together, and it had, in its own way. Still, Lewitt was hardly prone to intimate address. So Hollie looked.

"You know what a real emergency looks like," she began. "You know what it's like to wonder if you're going to survive the next five minutes or the next five hours or the next five days. Ask yourself if going back to your hometown to ensure the region is safe and protected is really an emergency situation." Another sigh. "I know what it's like to work hard, Hollie. Trust me. But you don't want to turn around in twenty years and realize you've done it all alone."

Damn Debra Lewitt for being as perceptive at reading people as she was at anticipating emergency fallouts.

Because even if Hollie could have denied it, even if she could have looked her discerning boss right in the eye and told her that Wolf Creek, Montana, was just a place and nothing more, she didn't get the chance. Lewitt tapped on the folder with one nail, raised her eyebrow and said, "Call me when you arrive on Sunday." Without another word, she turned on her heel and strode out of Hollie's office.

Be like Debra Lewitt and you might survive this. Might. Because as much as returning to a town she hadn't called home in nearly a decade wasn't the emergency she was used to, wasn't the fires and the floods and the tornados, it *was* an emergency. And when she thought about returning, about facing down the memories and emotions she had been running from faster than a cyclone on the open plains, Hollie couldn't help but wonder which was more dangerous.

Chapter One

And there goes the floor.

Sawyer always knew when the floor was about to collapse. In the din of the fire, the roar compounded by the fishbowl of his helmet and oxygen mask, he couldn't hear much beyond angry, sharp sounds of chaos, a wardrobe falling over, glass shattering. He never *heard* the floor beneath his feet begin to give, but he damn near almost always felt it, and it precipitated a real bad scene each and every time it had happened to him.

Time to move ass, Matthews.

Because they were missing one of the Hemwick children and he'd be damned if he let anything happen to the kid on his watch. But he'd already been inside the ranch house for two, maybe three minutes and they hadn't arrived on the scene for at least six or seven after the call had come in.

But Sawyer wasn't the type to play at odds. A wrong-side-of-the-tracks, school-paid-lunches kid like him knew that placing any sort of belief in a higher system

was bound to end in disaster. So he stuck to the cold —
hot — hard facts and to the very tangible things he could
do with the resources right in front of him.

Like walking down the hall and away from the
cracking floorboards. The door at the far end of the
hallway was shut and Sawyer hoped like hell that the
missing child was in that room, and not any of the three
open doorways he'd passed on his too-slow walk. If
they had been, he was too late. He got to the door after
what felt like an eternity and jangled the knob.

What's behind door number four?

Hopefully, April Anne Hemwick.

Heat from the blaze around him had warped the
wood and he came at it from the side, shoving the
weight of his body against the door until it finally
pushed free of the jamb. Thankfully, it didn't break,
and when one glance around the room told him that the
fire hadn't yet spread inside, he quickly pushed the
door closed again. The air was smoky and thick, but
there weren't any discernable flames and that gave him
hope. If April Anne had been in this room when the fire
started, she might just be okay.

Just as with the crunch of the floorboard beneath his
feet, it was intuition, instinct and experience, rather
than a discernable sound, that pulled him to the far
corner of the room. He crouched low and through the
haze caught sight of a flash of pink and blue. He tapped
her on the leg and she turned, *thank fuck*, and he
realized she was holding something. Two somethings.

Kittens. Fucking wonderful.

It was challenging enough bringing a four-year-old
down from the second story of a burning house, but
add kittens to the mix?

Doesn't matter.

It didn't matter. He lifted April Anne from the ground and pressed her face into his chest, the kittens squished between them, before walking three short steps to the window. Most of his team was down below and he pushed the window open easily enough, drawing attention to their position with a quick wave. One of the engines was brought quickly to the other side of the house and Jensen was practically halfway up the ladder by the time it hit the window. He took April Anne from Sawyer's arms and Sawyer scooped the two kittens from her hands so that she could properly hold on to Jensen on the descent. Then he, too, began climbing his way back down until he felt the hard, sold metal of the engine under his feet, then the ground below that.

By the time he got his helmet off, a challenge with the squirming kittens now both held by their scruffs in one hand, April Anne was in her mother's arms and the six Hemwicks had gathered together in a massive hug before turning to watch the second floor collapse and the house begin to implode right before their eyes.

"It's okay." Daniel Hemwick was holding his son's hand and stroking his wife's back. "We're all okay. The things are just things, but we still have each other."

It wasn't an unfamiliar sentiment to hear at a site like this one, but it still made something in Sawyer's belly clench in an uncomfortable way, and he tried not to focus on all the reasons that might be. Waiting until he would no longer interrupt the moment, he walked over to the family and knelt before April Anne, then extended the two kittens in his hand.

She pulled free of her mother's grip and caught him around the neck, hugging him so tightly that it nearly knocked Sawyer to his ass. This little girl had just gone

through hell and she still packed a powerful punch—
he only hoped he'd be so lucky one day.

"Thanks, Spider-Man," she said, then took the two
kittens and hugged them close before handing them to
her mother. He'd take Spiderman. It was one of the
most recent superhero blockbuster films, and with long
red hair and freckles to his hairline, he hardly passed
for the King of Wakanda. He pulled his gear off his
hand to ruffle her hair, then turned to her parents.

"I'm sorry about your house," Sawyer said. It was
true—he may have been a brusque, cynical s.o.b., but it
was hard to feel anything other than sympathy for a
family who had just lost so much.

"Nothing to be sorry about," Daniel Hemwick said.
He extended his hand and Sawyer was surprised to
find the man's grip was strong, despite everything their
family had experienced that night. "You saved our
April Anne. That's the only thing that matters, Chief."

The Spiderman praise from a four-year-old, he could
handle. This was edging on too gushy for him, but
Sawyer held the man's gaze, nodded to Jenny
Hemwick, whose eyes were glassy with unshed tears,
then turned away from the family to head back to his
engine. Jensen was sitting on the back bumper,
chugging a bottle of water, and he handed one to
Sawyer, who drank it down greedily.

Before they had the chance to exchange a word,
however, Jensen's eyes sparked at something behind
him and Sawyer's hackles rose.

"Chief." This was not said in the same tone that
Daniel Hemwick had used. Sawyer bit the inside of his
lip, not bothering to hide his grimace when he turned
to face Cade Easton.

Lewis and Clark County Sheriff Cade Easton was the
day to Sawyer's night, if day and night enjoyed

squirting each other in the eye with lemon juice and rubbing it in with salt. Where Sawyer's hair was long and red, Cade wore his just shy of military style. Where Sawyer made a habit of running into burning buildings—quite literally playing with fire—Cade ensured that law and order were upheld, to a nauseating degree in their tiny, nearly crimeless county. Cade was a stickler for rules Sawyer had never had any trouble breaking, and the only time Sawyer had seen him behave as anything less than a proper fucking gentleman was when he was poking at Sawyer's bruises that would otherwise have healed a long time ago.

"Sheriff." This in a very specific tone from Sawyer, who had very little difficulty stooping to Easton's level where pettiness was concerned.

"Glad to see the kittens of Wolf Creek remained unscathed," Easton said drily. "I have to get your statement."

Instead of replying, Sawyer took a long drink from the water bottle Jensen had handed him, taking some perverse pleasure in making the sheriff wait. Cade didn't need his statement right now any more than they needed a match, but he liked making a show of being the big gun in town, as if Sawyer's team were the cleanup crew and he owned the mansion.

"You'll get my statement tomorrow, Easton," Sawyer said after an intentionally long pause. "Just come on down to the station to pick it up."

Easton didn't miss a beat. "Now, Chief," he said. "Don't make this harder than it needs to be." They were in each other's faces now—for *fuck's* sake, how did they always end up in each other's faces?—and Sawyer only realized he was clenching his jaw when it began to throb in time with the pounding of his heart.

When did it get like this?

When had it gotten like this? They had never been friends, not really, but the stark animosity between them was a hell of a lot stronger now than it had been back in the beginning. Sure, two fucked-up kids from the wrong side of town were either gonna scuffle or have each other's backs, and it was clear that best friends they would never be, but it shouldn't have been this fucking hard to have a goddamn conversation without it nearly coming to blows.

You know exactly when it got to be like this.

Yeah, and Sawyer was about as likely to admit it as he was to get down on one knee and propose to Cade Easton.

"Did someone forget to take his happy pills today?" Sawyer prodded, taking perverse pleasure in watching the fury behind Easton's eyes. Running the Wolf County Fire Department took some of the edge off the rebellious streak that had plagued him since childhood, but pissing people off — especially Easton — was a goddamn fun way to pass the time.

"I'm not the one who needs happy pills. But if you want someone to buy your Viagra, you can just ask," Easton replied. "I'm sure we can get you back to rights no problem."

"Maybe if you spent half as much time running chasing down criminals as you do thinking about my dick, you'd feel better about yourself."

"I'd say you're stooping low, but word about town is that you're packing short," Easton replied with a smug grin.

Sawyer grunted to cover the laugh. It helped when his regular sparring partner was actually capable of delivering serious blows, and though he'd never admit aloud, Cade Easton could be one funny fuck. But before

Sawyer had the chance to think up some retort that would put an end to their inane bickering, he caught sight of a woman walking under the *caution* tape. His vision narrowed and Easton, Jensen and everything around them disappeared to background chatter. Nothing else mattered. Nothing else had ever mattered.

Hollie was back.

Chapter Two

Hollie had driven through the night to get from Denver to Wolf Creek, Montana, and she still hadn't been able to sleep when they'd arrived at the B&B located on the Triple Diamond Ranch. She'd spent the night tossing and turning, and three cups of coffee for breakfast and another one on the way out here meant she was extra jittery, extra jumpy and extra fidgety.

Sure, blame it on the coffee.

And not on a reunion she'd spent the better part of a decade doing her best to avoid. Her return to Wolf Creek had been hard enough — driving past the same old landmarks and new buildings and eateries that hadn't been there when she had left — but that was nothing in comparison to how challenging it was going to be to face the two men she had left behind without a word.

Could have done one-on-one…

She had considered it, meeting first with the sheriff then with the fire chief and saving their big old reunion together for absolutely *never*. But she was here to do a job, a job where people's lives, homes and livelihoods depended on her ability to make the right choice. And getting their very uncomfortable reunion over with *was* the right choice.

If you can jump out of a plane, you can do this. That thought wasn't very comforting. In fact, she was inclined to take the skydiving over walking across the lawn to where the two men stood at the back of Engine 64, obviously sniping at each other.

She must have tensed at the sight of them, because her field operations assistant, Savannah Walsh, glanced her way with a concerned expression. Savannah was smart as a whip and eleven times out of ten Hollie was glad to have her on her team, but she really didn't need the additional scrutiny right now, not for this conversation.

"Why don't you go introduce yourself to the Deputy Sheriff?" Hollie asked Savannah, rather than allowing her the opportunity to ask what kind of stick had just shoved itself up Hollie's ass. "She's the one over by the far patrol car." Hollie recognized Camilla Flores, but just barely. A few years younger than Hollie, Camilla had shown promise even back in middle school. Naturally, Hollie had been long gone before she'd ever really gotten to know the girl, but the woman, even at a distance, appeared capable and held herself with power and grace. She'd be a good ally to have in the fight against natural forces, Hollie had little doubt of that.

Savannah nodded and turned toward Camilla. Then Hollie didn't have any excuse, anything to keep her from walking the short distance across the lawn to where she would look down the barrel of her past from two different directions.

Shark cage diving in South Africa. Bungee jumping in Nepal.

Speaking with Cade and Sawyer for the first time in ten years.

One foot in front of the other, Hollie crossed the lawn, conscious that they had both turned to watch her approach, so utterly aware of them she felt as if her skin were burning behind the windbreaker, but what could she do about it? This was a bed she had made years ago and the time had come for her to nest.

"Chief, Sheriff." She stopped before them both, standing equal parts away from where Sawyer lazed on the bumper of his engine and Cade stood with his stance wide and his arms crossed. The poses, the looks, the discerning gazes, were all so indicative of who these men had been back then that Hollie almost felt as if no time had passed at all. Though, of course, so very much had.

"Hollie Callihan, as I live and breathe." Sawyer spoke first. She would have recognized his voice anywhere, but now it was darker, richer, just like the long swirls of red hair curling at his shoulders and the thick beard that framed his face. His freckles were still there, dark and reaching all the way to his hairline, and Hollie found herself thinking the unimaginable stupid gratitude of *thank God*. She'd always loved his freckles. They gave softness to a man built of hard edges and dark lines—a hardness she'd only ever added to.

Fuck, I'd like to add to that hardness right now.

Fuck, indeed.

"What are you doing here, Hollie?"

She turned to face Cade, and the heat rising in her chest, the need that had terrified her just as much as all the rest of it, did just about the opposite of abate. Cade's words were less harsh, less mean-spirited, but they weren't kind or gentle either—not that she had expected them to be, not after all this time, not after the way she had left things.

But, *damn it*, it hurt to look at him, to look at both of them, different as the sea and the sky and yet both such fundamental parts of who she was, both her biggest regret, both the dusty memories she unpacked late at night, alone in an empty apartment, wondering if she was going to pay for her sins with a stark home and starker bed for the rest of her life.

"I'm here on business," she said, squaring her shoulders and pitching her voice low. She had learned at Debra Lewitt's side, after all, and Hollie had seen that woman eat senators for breakfast. "The Denver office of FEMA, to be exact."

Sawyer let out a low whistle. "Of course."

Cade was more forthcoming. "What kind of business is FEMA doing in Wolf Creek, Agent?" he asked. She'd done that. She had put that harshness into his voice. She had made Cade Easton sound so mean.

"Keeping it above water, Sheriff," she said, her voice blessedly without a waver or hitch. "We have projections that the next two weeks of snowmelt runoff from the Black Reefs are going to do some serious damage, and we're looking to take preventative measures."

Both of them stiffened at that, though Hollie honestly hadn't believed any more tension could have been added to the moment. This was a different kind, though, one that had everything to do with the need these men both had to protect the people in their town and nothing to do with the last night they had seen one another.

"We have history." She made a point of reaching first Sawyer's green gaze, then Cade's dark brown one, before continuing. "I'm not opposed to clearing the air, if that's what it takes to make this operation go as smoothly as possible. But I am here to do a job and it requires both of you. As of this moment, I am acting superior for the region and I will make every effort to act as professionally as possible. I only ask that both of you do the same."

The silence after her speech was weighty and Hollie actually felt the heat rising from her chest to her cheeks. She hadn't been this terrified in years. Not since she had been back in this godforsaken town, wondering what in the hell to do next.

"We're not little boys anymore, Hollie," Cade said, and though his voice was quiet, it was anything but soft. "At least, some of us aren't." He shot a pointed glance at Sawyer, and Hollie couldn't help but wonder if something was going on between them that she didn't know about. "I can tell you I'll do whatever it takes to keep Wolf Creek safe." His voice was resolute, a stronger, more confident, more capable version of the man she had left behind.

More everything, if the way he filled out that uniform was anything to go by.

And if she couldn't keep those intrusive and unwelcome thoughts to herself it was going to be a long two weeks.

"Much as I hate to agree with Easton on anything," Sawyer put in, his tone more prodding, more pushing for a reaction, "I took on the responsibility of keeping this town safe. And I'll do it." He stood up at that and Hollie was suddenly all too aware of how tall he was, of how broad he had become in the last few years. Even though his gear was bulky, she could still make out the strength of his body and the power behind his stature. "But if you're expecting me to be the same man you left behind, you can forget it. Apologize all you want, Hollie. Talk until you're blue in the face. It's too late to change anything between us."

He picked up his helmet and started walking away. "Call me when you're ready to discuss emergency preparations. And not before."

And just like that, he was gone.

Hypocrite.

She turned back to Cade, but his expression was just as inscrutable as the back of Sawyer's head had been.

"It's been a long time, Hollie," he said quietly. "Your life may have changed, but time moves slower in Wolf Creek, you know that. It won't just be a matter of coming back and returning to the way things were." He took a step away from her and paused. Then a slow, barely there smile turned up the corners of his lips.

"It may be hell for me to see you right now, Hollie Callihan, but damn if it ain't a little bit of heaven too."

Then he was gone, leaving Hollie standing alone behind Engine 64.

You're wrong, Cade. My life never changed so much I forgot you two. And it never could.

But before she got the chance to live the rest of her life trying to ignore the deep pang she felt in her heart, she was going to have to get through the next two weeks — and neither Cade nor Sawyer seemed willing to make it easy for her.

Nothing less than I deserve.

Chapter Three

"Sheriff, you ready to leave in a few minutes?" Deputy Sheriff Camilla Flores knocked on the open door to his office at the same time she walked inside and Cade finally put down the climate reports he wasn't reading. Cam was as good a distraction as any, considering his mind had been doing somersaults for the last three hours and no amount of coffee breaks or paperwork had been able to bring him back to task — no matter that they were predicting severe flooding in the next two weeks.

Hollie was back in Wolf Creek.

Hollie Callihan, the woman who had left Cade all those years ago and had taken a healthy chunk of his heart with her. Cade wasn't exactly used to people sticking around, but he'd known Hollie in a way he'd known so few other people — and she had known him.

Or so he had thought.

But it had been nearly ten years and she was back here, more confident, more capable and more ready for battle than she had ever been.

The memory of watching her stride across the lot made his mouth go dry. Her regulation windbreaker hadn't afforded him a view of the curves he only knew she had grown into, but her hair was shorter and lighter, curling at the end as it had hung from a tight ponytail. Her minimal makeup had only highlighted those discerning blue eyes and soft, full mouth—a mouth Cade knew all too well.

A mouth that had him hardening in an instant, and he thanked God that he was still behind his desk.

"Sheriff." Cam's voice was not amused. "Cade, you still here with me?"

Decidedly not, but Cam had the nasty habit of actually caring about the people in her life, and she always seemed to know when Cade hadn't gone home to sleep or hadn't eaten a real meal in three days. Without a word, she would have three pans of tamales or enchiladas or empanadas sitting in his fridge the next day. And since Martina Flores, Camilla's mother, was much better cook than Cade, he gratefully accepted them.

But right now even the prospect of homemade *bunuelos* wasn't enough to keep Cade from thinking about the way Hollie had felt in his arms all those years ago. In fairness, there had never really been a time when he hadn't been thinking about how Hollie felt in his arms, but seeing her here again in the flesh brought it all back into multicolor and had Cade questioning just about everything he knew.

"It's Hollie, isn't it?" Camilla's keen eye and protective nature made her a damn good deputy, but it also meant she stuck her nose where it most definitely didn't belong.

"That obvious?" Cade asked, raking his hand through his hair—or trying, at least. His latest—and shortest—haircut had essentially put an end to that habit.

"You look like you've seen a ghost," Camilla agreed. "But, like, a ghost you're really mad at."

Was he angry with Hollie? Sawyer certainly was, but Cade knew Sawyer Matthews well enough to know that the man was all about putting on a show. Still, the vehemence in the other man's eyes…

Cade understood. In fact, he might have been the only person in the world who did. But angry? Not really. Not anymore. The hurt was still real. The sadness. The regret. But he had seen first-hand what anger did to men—even those that had once been decent and good-hearted, and he had done his damnedest to keep his own emotions deeply in check. Except for where Sawyer was concerned, but they had their own set of history that took a different kind of a dealing with.

And how will you deal with Hollie?

He had a couple of ideas and none of them had to do with anger.

"It's been a long time," Cade admitted. "You think I'd be past it by now, but…" He trailed off. Cam knew him well enough to make her own assumptions—he certainly didn't need to give her all the details.

"It doesn't work like that, Hoss," she said, pushing off the door frame and coming fully into the room. "Jillian and I broke up six years ago and I still love her. If you have something unresolved with Hollie, of course you're feeling confused." Confused was an understatement if Cade had ever heard one, but Cam so rarely mentioned her ex-girlfriend that he knew she was doing her best to tread lightly around his feelings. Which he *really* didn't want her to do. He might have been many things, but he sure as hell wasn't fragile.

"I'll be fine," he said, standing from his desk and shrugging into his jacket. It was spring, but this was Montana and the weather didn't listen to the calendar. Camilla's look said she was having none of his nonsense, but also that she knew better than to speak the words out loud.

Cade should have known better. He should have known that the first woman—the only woman he had ever fallen in love with—would leave him eventually. He should have known by senior year of high school that the only person in the world he could count on was himself. He should have known all those things, but Hollie had taken him far away from Wolf Creek. She had made him feel like someone worth the effort. She had given him a chance to succeed, whether she knew it or not. Then she had left, only after he'd been given just enough hope to have his heart broken.

"How about you let me drive, Sheriff?" Camilla asked. Cade pushed the thoughts of Hollie, of their past, of everything that had happened between them, far away. He was not going to let her arrival distract him from his most important job—keeping the people of Wolf Creek safe. So he shook his head, climbed into the driver's seat and set off to do his job—beautiful blondes with knowing eyes and adventure in their hearts be damned.

* * * *

"Hollie Callihan, come here and give us a hug."

Hollie couldn't overstate the relief she felt at spying the friendly faces of Dec McCormick and Micah Ellison. Half the town seemed gathered on the open stretches of field beyond the Triple Diamond Ranch B&B, which the owner, Maddy Hollis, had graciously allowed them to use as a point location for emergency response. Hollie weaved through the crowd and came to stand before the tall men, tilting her head up to meet their eyes.

"It's great to see you guys," she managed, before Dec engulfed in her a hug, then Micah gave her a much more subdued welcome, though his smile was no less pleased or welcoming. "It's been a hell of a time back here, I'll tell you that." Because all she had done since arriving had been to look her past dead in the eyes and, *fuck*, if her past didn't look a hell of a lot more delicious than it had when she'd left.

"Does that mean our esteemed fire captain and sheriff will be all the more delightful to work with?" Dec asked with an all-too-knowing grin. Hollie elbowed him in the gut.

"That's none of your business. And you know I'm not about rehashing the events of that night." *That night* being the time Hollie's Search and Rescue team, back before she had entered the ranks of the bureaucracy, had teamed up with Black Reef S&R to rescue a field trip of overnight campers who had been stranded during a flash flood. Dec was a few years older than her, but they'd made the Wolf Creek connection in an instant, and she'd become just as friendly with his search partner, Micah.

After rescuing the students and their two shaken but impressively capable chaperones, the three of them, along with several others, had gotten rip-roaring drunk at the hotel bar and Hollie had let a few important pieces of information slip.

Though she'd remained in good touch with Micah and Dec over the years, especially as they had expanded their S&R training camp and she'd risen through the ranks in the emergency response field, they never, ever mentioned what she had spoken of that night — or how her relationship with Cade Easton and Sawyer Matthews was complicated on a good day and downright disastrous on a bad one.

"As long as you're keeping a good head on your shoulders," Dec said, giving her a once-over that felt nearly identical to the one Wes had given her last time he'd been home from South America.

"Don't get all big brother on me," Hollie said, taking a step back. "I may make a habit of jumping out of planes, but no part of me plans to take that route while I'm back here."

Dec's lips twisted, but he didn't say anything else, for which Hollie was grateful. It was bad enough that she was back here, bad enough that she had to see Cade and Sawyer. The fewer people who knew, the fewer people who could make underhanded comments or pass judgments, the better. Not that she expected Dec McCormick to pass judgments. Neither he nor Micah was the type. But she was back in Wolf Creek as a grown adult, and the time for mind games and fantasies was well past.

"Hollie, I'd love for you to meet someone," Dec said, interrupting her quickly derailing internal monologue. "We both would."

Hollie turned and spied a beautiful brunette standing between Dec and Micah. She was tall, which meant a lot considering both men were well over six feet, and she had a shine in her eyes and a smile on her lips that would have made her pretty even if her long hair hadn't been sleek and soft freckles hadn't dusted her nose and cheeks.

"This is Lily Hollis — she's the new park ranger for Black Reef and her sister owns the Triple Diamond." Dec paused and glanced down at Lily Hollis with an expression of pure, unadulterated love, and something in Hollie's heart swelled and deflated all at the same time.

"She's ours, Hollie," Micah finished. Beside him, Dec continued to gaze longingly into her eyes and Lily just smiled. "Both of ours."

The way he said the words was so simple, so calm and casual and basic, that it took Hollie a full moment to register their meaning. She had lived in three countries, more than a dozen cities, experienced unique cultures, foods and languages and yet, it still came as a slow shock, like rising too quickly from a dive and feeling the lightheadedness start to set in. She looked at Lily again.

"It's a lot to take in, I know," Lily said with a genuine smile. "I wish I could say I thought of it first, but my sister gets all the credit." She popped up on her tiptoes and indicated a cluster of people, where Maddy Hollis, the woman who had checked Hollie in the night before, stood with two men. "She inherited the ranch and she got everything came with it." Everything being Christian Harlow and Ryder Dean, two boys who'd been a few years older than Hollie in school and who'd had a reputation as troublemaking and heartbreaking.

"She converts people too," Dec said on a laugh. "We made friends with a couple of federal agents that were here back in January. One conversation with Lily…" He trailed off, or maybe her ears had just stopped working, because there was no way…

There's always been a way.

It was a thought that had haunted her for years, a fantasy, the imagining of a desperate girl who would never even try to realize what she wanted. Even though she wasn't afraid, not of heights or insects or public speaking, *God*, she was so very afraid of this.

"Hollie." It wasn't until Lily placed her arm on Hollie's shoulder that Hollie had even realized her train of thought had left the station. "I do hope this isn't going to prevent us from becoming friends." Her voice was soft and sweet, but Hollie didn't doubt for a second that the woman was made of something stronger, something Hollie had never been made of.

"Not at all," she said quickly. "I'm happy my friends are happy. If it's a little unconventional, that doesn't bother me." It did, however, bring back fantasies she'd long repressed, fantasies of how that night might have gone, of too many hands, too many bodies, of writhing against hot, hard muscle, the kind to which she had compared every lover and experience to follow.

"I'm glad you see it that way," Lily said brightly. "Wolf Creek is such an open community. There's been a lot less blowback than I expected." She indicated toward the ridge and Hollie kept pace with her as they moved away from the crowd.

"Dec is right about Ev," she said, when they were a short distance away and only Hollie could make out what she was saying. "Ev had answers to questions she didn't know how to ask and it so happened that we were here to help her make sense of things." She turned and gave Hollie a look that made her feel like a blinking neon sign with every thought and emotion in multicolor display on her forehead. "I saw the expression on your face when the guys introduced me, and I just wanted to say that if you're ever in a situation where you need...well, whatever it may be, look us up. We get it."

Hollie couldn't help herself. She threw her arms around Lily's neck and hugged her before pulling back, laughing slightly.

"I'll never, ever need those kinds of answers," she said. "But God, it feels so good to have a friend here. I haven't been home… I haven't been back in Wolf Creek in a long time."

Lily's smile was genuine, but before the conversation could develop further, Savannah came jogging up, her dark red hair swishing in a ponytail behind her.

"Sheriff just pulled up, which means we're all set to get started," she said. She typed out a few things on the tablet in her hand, then passed it over to Hollie. Hollie nodded, gave Lily one last smile and returned to the clearing of tents. With the S&R teams, fire department and sheriff's department, there were about thirty people clustered before her, and she stepped up on a chair to gather their attention.

"Thank you all so much for joining us," Hollie began, amazed to hear that her voice was calm, solid, without a hitch or waver. This was what she was good at. Analyzing how more than one relationship in this tiny town had turned out so…unconventional was *not* what she was good at, and it was a decidedly dangerous path to tread, given the history looming behind her. But standing before heroes and heroines and preparing for an emergency, that she could handle.

"We're going to divide Lewis and Clark County into five districts. Flash floods are expected in districts two and four, with critical infrastructure systems in districts two and three." Savannah handed her the printed map and she indicated the locations while she spoke, the group responsive and engaged. They were professional rescuers, most of them, conditioned to work in extreme environments and all too familiar with the location and terrain. Whatever Mother Nature had in store for them, Hollie knew they would be able to see it through to the other end with minimal damage.

As for herself...

Hollie glanced out into the crowd of firefighters, police officers, a few friendly faces — Dec and Micah among them — people she recognized from growing up here, from living here, from being a part of Wolf Creek.

And Cade.

And Sawyer.

It was hard not to recognize them.

Cade stood at the edge of the circle, his body stiff, his attention fixed on her and the notebook in his hand. He was taller than she remembered, certainly more muscled, and with a good pair of blue jeans on he could have been the consummate Captain America, all power and respect and a sense of duty that shone through in his dark brown gaze, in the way he held himself.

Sawyer lazed against the world — and against the side of his Jeep, legs crossed at the ankles, hair curling against his shoulders like shining red jewels. He was gruff and ready to fight, if the tattoos curling up both arms and peeking out from the crew neck of his shirt, and the dark black studs in his ears, were anything to go by.

They've grown up quite nicely.

A thought that would surely be her undoing.

But as Hollie continued her presentation and kept half an eye on both men she had been avoiding for so long, there was one irrefutable truth. Wolf Creek might survive the storm unscathed, what with this team keeping watch, but there was no way Hollie would make it back home in one piece.

Chapter Four

Sawyer wasn't about to call it sulking. Hell, he never sulked. He drank and partied and put up a Devil-May-Go-Fuck-Himself persona until he'd been well and truly left alone, then he squashed whatever pesky emotions might have made him sulk way down deep until all that was left was the hard, shiny shell and a lot of expensive ink.

And since he was not sulking, that meant he was in the barn to see if his Dr. Doolittle skills had kicked in or Narnia was hidden behind some saddle bags and extra bales of hay.

Next time Annabelle asks me to babysit, we're skipping story time. Not that Sawyer would ever skip story time if his niece looked at him with those baby blues of hers, but she was clearly making him soft, and if there was ever a time to have his battle armor on...

He leaned over the edge of one of the gates, where a dark brown foal sat folded up in a pile of limbs, watching him with discerning eyes. *Fine.* He'd take the creepily human gaze from the young horse over standing out in the field, trying to focus on his job, when Hollie *fucking* Callihan was just a few feet away.

Hollie.

He couldn't hate her. He'd tried for so long to hate her and it simply hadn't worked. Hell, he didn't even hate Cade, though he'd never admit it aloud. It was just...

She had been the first woman he had ever loved. She had made him a better man — hell, she had made him a man where others had failed. Then she'd disappeared into the mist without a trace, leaving the two of them behind to make heads and tails of what had happened and how to move forward.

A rustle near the door caught his attention and when Sawyer turned, he couldn't keep from swearing under his breath. Thinking about Hollie hadn't summoned her all those years ago and it didn't summon her on the lonely nights he spent in his empty bed, but apparently practice made perfect, because there she was in the flesh right before him.

Looking more beautiful than ever.

More dangerous than ever.

"I'm sorry," she said, tripping slightly over the words, a faint flush spreading across her cheeks. Gone was the powerful emergency responder she had been just a few moments before. Gone was the woman who had dared them all to jump from the highest cliffs in the Black Reef Mountains to the waters below, taking the leap herself before anyone else got the chance. She was just a woman, standing there looking like she didn't have a clue what to do next. "I didn't realize anyone was in here. I'll leave you to it."

"Hollie, wait." Sawyer didn't know what in the fuck had prompted him to say that. The less time he spent with Hollie, the better off they would all be. Still, he'd never been able to stand seeing her sad in all the years he had known her, and the idea that she felt vulnerable, exposed because of him wrenched something in Sawyer he hadn't realized was still wrenchable. "You can stay. If you want."

Her expression changed as if to tell him, point blank, that he was half the reason she was looking for cover. Still, she took a step farther into the barn, then another, until the door swung shut behind her and Sawyer caught her scent against the hay and wool of the bar. She was floral, just like the early spring outside — more a breath of fresh air than an overabundance of flowers, but beautiful and potent in her own right.

And though he ached hard with outright frustration and pain and anger, part of him *burned* for that scent, for the way she had felt in his arms, for how she would always be his spring that would never come. He had a lifetime of April showers waiting for him and lusting after Hollie Callihan wasn't going to make them any easier to bear.

"Sawyer." She paused. Shoved her hands into her pockets. Leaned against the wooden gate behind her.

"I'm going to need more than that," he said, his tone rough and angry. She didn't appear shocked by it. "You've been gone a hell of a long time, Hollie. Things aren't the same now as when you left and, frankly, I don't think there's ever going to be a space for you to go back to the way they were."

Her shoulders sagged and he hated himself just a little bit for saying it, hated that he hated himself for it when her absence had been his greatest torment for years.

"I'm not here to stay," she said defiantly. "I'm here to do my job, just like you." She looked down at her feet. "Congratulations, by the way. On making captain. I know how much it meant to you."

She knew, because they had spent nights under the stars sharing their hopes and dreams. And she knew because he had told her—the one person he had ever told—that he was going to make something of himself one day. And she knew, because she had supported him.

For a while, at least.

"And you," he said, after a long moment. "Never pictured you for the office-job type, but I can see how skydiving and parasailing can get boring."

She shot him a wry grin and shook her head.

"I never stopped doing any of those things. But I needed the stability and I like helping people. Surely you can understand that."

Without question, but the idea of Hollie in an office still sat upside down for him. Then again, he didn't know this version of her, hadn't known her in a very long time.

"I hope you're happy, Sawyer," she said quietly. "Truly."

I was before you showed up.

Bitchy, but true. He'd been happy enough and not questioning what it would be like to find true and everlasting love, until she'd arrived and poured a shot-glass-worth of salt into what should have been a healed-over wound.

"Annabelle's married," he said instead. "Two kids. They're building a new house near Holter Lake."

She smiled. "I'm glad to hear it. Wes won't be, but he lost his chance." Because there was something about the Callihan clan and the Matthews clan that was forever entangled and entwined, even though Annabelle was only half-Matthews, out of the house before Sawyer had even really been a person, and Wes Callihan had never been one to find solid ground for longer than he had to.

"How's he doing?" Sawyer *hated* this, hated the stilted conversation with a woman he'd felt closer to than everyone else in the world. But what else was he supposed to say?

"Wes is good," Hollie said slowly. "He's going back to South America for another tour with the Peace Corps. I think he's teaching this time."

What Hollie didn't say, what she didn't need to say because Sawyer knew from nothing more than the look in her eyes and the tone of her voice, was that she was lonely. Just like Hollie, her brother was an adventurer, forever throwing darts at a map to see what hit. But Hollie had a domestic, cozy streak about her that might have accounted for the desk job in a way Wes never had. And when she had very intentionally lost track of Wolf Creek, Hollie had been forced to start over, to make entirely new friends and connections.

"This is hard," she said after a moment. "Being back. Seeing you and…seeing you all grown up and living your dream. I'm so happy for you, Sawyer, truly. But it's going to be a long two weeks."

Understatement of the century if I ever heard one, but she already knew that. And since he was feeling generous, Sawyer was willing to concede that Hollie didn't just have one piece of her past to contend with. She had two. Entirely of her own doing, of course, but still.

"It's not easy for me either," he said, glancing to the toe of his boot, which had never been interesting before this moment. Finally, he looked back up, caught her eye and stroked his beard. Her gaze followed the moment of his hand and he almost, *almost* smiled. He'd been a rough and scraggly ginger of a kid, and the only reason he'd avoided a solid bully beat down every other day of the week was because he'd learned how to fight early on, how to keep people off his back—most people, at least—and how to hold his own. Last she had seen him, the hair on the top of his head had been short and the beard had been shorter—full, but at eighteen, not yet something to be proud of.

"You like the beard?" It was inane because *what the fuck, Matthews,* and also because it was a pickup line he'd used a few too many times in a few too many bars. Women almost always liked the beard, liked the ink and liked the muscles under his firefighter gear.

"You're so grown up," she managed, and though her voice was wistful, laced with nostalgia and sadness, those words made heat curl in his belly and an ache spread though his body. Part of him wanted her to turn around, walk out of that door and never come back. Part of him wanted to show Hollie Callihan exactly how grown up he was.

"You haven't changed in the slightest," he replied instead, hearing the gravel in his voice and hoping to fuck she didn't. She raised her eyebrow and Sawyer just managed to keep a straight face. She was, of course, more beautiful than ever, her skin golden from a lifetime of adventures he hadn't been invited on, wisps of hair escaping her ponytail and framing her face, those discerning dark blue eyes. Her eyes had always reminded him of the ocean—calm, but because they wanted to be, and oh so capable of wreaking havoc on a man.

She took a step forward, then another one, and Sawyer had to wonder how it was this, her nearness, the way her hand trembled at her side as if she were struggling not to reach up and cup his face, that made his heart pound so wildly and his mind feel so out of control where running into burning buildings never had.

"I missed you," she said. Her voice was quiet but the statement seemed to echo around the barn as if she had shouted into her emergency megaphone. "Just thought you should know." She turned to leave, but Sawyer grabbed her wrist.

"No." His pulse was burning through his veins now, pumping blood as quickly as the rapids in the valley below. She faced him, her expression curious, almost anticipatory, as if she didn't have any better idea how this was going to play out than he did.

"No?"

"No, Hollie." He tugged her closer, trying to ignore how smooth her skin felt below his calloused fingers as she willingly moved into his space. "No, you don't get to waltz back in here after ten *fucking* years and tell me that you missed me without an explanation. No, you don't get to start putting crazy ideas in my head after all the time I'd spent thinking about you and no, goddamn it, you don't get to stand there looking so beautiful it makes me regret every choice I've ever made."

His voice was a low growl and he was giving over to the anger with such ease that he knew he needed to pull back, knew he needed to stop before too many words got out, before too many things were left hanging in the air between them, unable to pushed back into the box.

"It's not just about you." She said this flatly and he would have believed it, had her pulse not been fluttering where he still held her wrist. God, it would be so easy, so delicious, to just turn and press her against the barn wall, to pin both of her slender wrists in one of his hands and to…

"Of course." He dropped her hand, as the words began to register. There had been a catalyst for when he and *Sheriff* Easton had gone from casual friends to sworn enemies.

"Can you give me time, Sawyer?" she asked him. This time, she stepped forward all on her own and those extra few inches pushed hard at the foundation of Sawyer's self-control. He needed to put an end to this right now. He needed to send her on her way and make sure she kept her distance for the next two weeks.

But then she put her hands on his chest and the bare touch of her fingers against the fabric of his shirt made Sawyer's mouth go dry and his mind go blank. He had fantasized over her touch for nearly a decade and there simply wasn't any restraint left.

"Just a little bit of time to figure out how to explain. *Shit.*" She shook her head and those soft blonde waves brushed against his shirt too, tickled the exposed skin of his neck, made him want to wrap his hand around the base of her ponytail and pull *hard*. His cock tightened at the thought, growing painfully rigid behind his jeans, and it took everything in him not to release the groan that her simple touch, her nearness, caused.

Not that it would have made much of a difference, because Hollie had her head tilted downward, and when she lifted her gaze to look at him, her cheeks were flushed bright pink.

Wonderful. There's nothing like classic heartbreak, lust and humiliation.

Still she didn't step away. In fact, it seemed to Sawyer almost as if she were moving closer, closing the small space between them one half inch at a time. Surely that was his crazed imagine speaking. Surely she wasn't looking at him with a glint of danger just sharp enough to cut the last threads of his self-control.

"Sawyer." His name wasn't even out of her lips when he pulled their bodies together and kissed her hard, fierce, demanding. Hollie Callihan was not a woman to back down from a challenge and she responded a second later with the same intensity that rioted through his own body, until he felt the wall behind his back and her lush form pressed against his front. His cock was screaming now, throbbing hard into the lush curve of her inner thigh, and it was all Sawyer could do to keep only kissing her, slipping his tongue in between her lips, ravaging and exploring her mouth and letting her do the same to him, even as he knew this was just about the worst choice he could have had made in a lifetime of regrets and poor choices.

"*Fuck*, Hollie." Was that his own voice? It was hard to tell, especially when the words got caught on a groan the moment she brushed his hard-on. Damn, this woman had the ability to turn his brain to mush in five seconds flat.

She moaned into his mouth and started trailing her hands across his chest, slowly, deliberately, caressing the muscles below his shirt, pausing at each erect nipple to tease and tantalize until they formed stiff peaks and his cock was hard enough to break stone. She was just moving lower, just pulling the shirt from his waistband, when a noise at the door startled them both.

"Hollie, are you in here? The press needs us down by the courthouse in…oh…"

In the dim light, Sawyer recognized the woman who had come out to Wolf Creek with Hollie, an Agent…something. At the moment, he didn't really give a damn. All he cared about was the way Hollie's breasts felt in his hands.

"Right," Hollie called back across the barn, her voice swollen and thick. *Because of me.* "I'll be out in just a moment, Van. Tell them to hold on."

The door was open and shut and they were both alone again, the spell indisputably broken and the power this woman held over him back to being shackles instead of wings.

"I'm sorry," she said, stepping back from him and pulling the ponytail tight against her scalp. She pushed those lovely strands of hair off her face and adjusted her shirt. "I shouldn't have put you in that position. It won't happen again."

And before Sawyer got the chance to tell her how very much he would like to be put back into that position, she followed her agent out of the door and left him standing in the barn alone.

Fool me once…

Chapter Five

So much for survival skills.

It hardly mattered that she'd spent the better part of a decade working search and rescue, hiking, diving, jumping and climbing. Forget the EMT training, First Aid training, CPR training and Emergency Response training. She might as well have slathered bacon grease all over her naked body and walked into a literal lion's den with the amount of survival prowess she had just exhibited.

But God, Sawyer had been standing there looking broody and beautiful, his eyes dark, his every muscle pulled taut, enticing. And she'd lost her fucking mind. Without question. Because kissing Sawyer Matthews in a dark barn one hundred feet away from half their town not two days after arriving back in Wolf Creek was, irrefutably, insane.

And yet, Hollie couldn't deny, not to herself, not in this moment of stark vulnerability, that it held felt so right to be back in his arms, touching the man that

Sawyer Matthews had become, feeling him, giving in to the pull that had scared her for so long.

If only it were that easy.

Because if it were just Sawyer, just her best friend, just the boy she had shared starry nights and mornings at the diner with, it would be one thing. If it were just Sawyer, she would never have run away with her tail between her legs and her mind unable to comprehend the maddening things she so desperately craved. If it were just Sawyer.

But it hadn't been just Sawyer back then, not even when he was ink-free and beardless and a foot shorter than the beautiful and base man she had just launched herself at in the barn. It hadn't been just Sawyer then and it wasn't just Sawyer now either.

"Do you mind if we take a little detour?" she asked Savannah. After her disastrous encounter in the barn, she had fled — again — grabbed Savannah and booked it for the press conference down by the courthouse. A quick meeting with the mayor had followed and she had been blissfully, beautifully, wonderfully distracted from the way Sawyer had felt below her fingertips, how his body had pressed against hers, lit her up from the inside out and made her forget every reason for leaving.

But now that she was navigating the old, familiar roads she'd taken so many times in her life, the distraction behind her, his touch, was all she could think about.

"Sure," Savannah eyed her curiously. "If you tell me what I walked in on in the barn this morning."

"Nothing to tell."

Liar, liar, regulation cargo pants on fire.

"Hollie." Savannah turned in her seat and Hollie glanced over at her. Savannah's bright, discerning eyes made the farm girl from Kansas too smart for her own good — far too smart for Hollie's good. But there was genuine concern there and Hollie couldn't help but sigh. She hadn't spoken to anyone about anything that had happened the night she had left Wolf Creek, except for that one drunken slip to Dec and Micah. Not even Wes, who had been on his second tour with the Peace Corps by then, knew the reason she had never gone back. But Savannah was a friend, a good one, someone she could rely on. Plus, the woman was going to get some information out of her sooner or later.

"You've been jumpy and fidgety since we got here," Savannah continued. "It's not like you to hook up with strangers, especially not on a job." Her gaze sharpened. "I want to know what to watch out for."

Hollie's heart softened slightly. It felt good to have someone watching her back. For so long it had been her against the world. Sure, she had her teams, her search and rescue partners and all the rest. But she'd never really stayed long enough in one place to make true friends — and if that had anything do with what she had so desperately wanted from the ones she had made once upon a time, Hollie wasn't going to give it a second thought.

"You're dangerous," she said with a smile. "I'm glad you're on my side."

Savannah gave her a grin, softening her freckles and making some of the loose red hair around her face spill in front of her eyes. *Lord save me from redheads with knowing gazes.*

"Okay. Information for detour. Fine." She took a deep breath at the same moment as she turned down the old, familiar road. "I grew up here, in Wolf Creek. Born and raised, actually."

Savannah didn't say a word, but out of the corner of her eye, Hollie saw the other woman raise her eyebrow.

"I left when I was eighteen and I never looked back. My grandmother had passed away and my brother was long gone, somewhere in South America or some such. I didn't have anything to tie me here."

If your nose gets any longer, you won't be able to see the road in front of you.

"It doesn't seem that way," Savannah said bluntly. Because she had, of course, seen Hollie sucking face with the fire captain just that morning.

"It's complicated, Van," she said quietly. "Sawyer... Sawyer was my best friend. But..." The old oak tree came into view and whatever she was going to say next died on Hollie's lips when she pulled up to the base of it and put the car into park. Savannah must have known, must have understood on some fundamental level, because she didn't say a word when Hollie got out of the car and slowly made her way across the lawn.

The grass was neatly trimmed, the paint slightly lighter than the baby blue it had been in her memories. The rope on the tire swing hanging from the far branch was fraying and the flowerbeds were empty, but fresh mulch and clean rocks showed good maintenance, good care. *It should be.* She paid a pretty penny to keep the place up, even though she'd never had any plans of returning, even though standing here, before this beautiful, classic, historic little house, was like stepping into a photograph, a film of her own life she had never planned to watch.

She walked slowly around to the back of the house. This had always been her favorite part, watching the way the backyard of her home had opened up to the wide, forever skies. Soft, flat clouds lazed overhead and she tilted her head back up to watch them, wondering, if only for a moment, how she could have left this all behind.

Fear of hurting the two people you care most about in the world.

But she had hurt them. She had hurt them and she had hurt herself. Running hadn't been a better way, just a different way, and it had meant giving up so much of who she was.

'She's ours. Both of ours.'

The way Micah had said that about his relationship, about Lily, about Dec McCormick, a man's man if Hollie had ever known one, it had tripped something up inside her, given her ideas she had no right to be thinking.

If she could return, if she could walk right back into her life here in Wolf Creek and indulge those deep, hidden secrets, would she?

It doesn't matter. Because you won't get the chance.

And pretending she would get the chance would only make it all the harder when she inevitably got up and walked away.

Cade spied Hollie's Jeep down the long dirt road and turned before he could think better of it. Chances were good she was staring up at the sky in the middle of her backyard, and part of him, a deeply hidden, desperately glutton for punishment part of him, needed to see that one last time.

"You forget something at home?" Camilla asked him from the passenger seat. She knew this drive all too well, for the same reason Cade knew that Hollie's room was the third window on the second floor, and for the same reason he just knew she was standing with her eyes closed to the sun and her arms stretched out.

They'd been so much more than next door neighbors.

And Hollie's grandmother had been so much more than his friend's guardian, Wes Callihan so much more than a passing acquaintance. The Callihan family had been the closest thing Cade had to a family, when his parents had spent their nights at bars outside of Helena doing God only knew what, and it was late night television and school lunches that had kept Cade fed and company.

He pulled up beside the forest green Jeep Cherokee and nodded to Agent Walsh, sitting in the front seat and looking through a pile of papers.

"Mind keeping Agent Walsh company for a moment?" he asked Cam, who gave him the look that told him she knew exactly what the fuck was going on and she was letting him get away with it. "She's pretty, Cam. It could be worse." He stepped out of the car and headed around back, aware Agent Walsh was watching him and that she was very much watching Cam, who had come around to the other side of the car. His feet followed the worn path almost without conscious thought and when he cleared the back of the house, there she was.

Hollie's hair was loose, spilling down her back in soft, shiny gold curls when she tilted her head skyward. Even without seeing it, Cade knew her eyes were closed, and he moved as quietly as he could to stand by her side. Her hand was close, fingers so very, very close to his own and he brushed their knuckles together as gently as he could, fearful of pulling her from her trance.

She must have known he was there, must have acted on the same instinct that had brought him back here, because her fingers wrapped around his own — smooth, soft, slightly calloused on the knuckles, but so familiar that it burned a path right up his body.

How many times had they stood here, just like this, eyes closed, hands held tight, faces tilted up to the skies? When she spoke, her voice was soft as the touch of her fingertips.

"How did you know I would be here?" It wasn't an accusation, merely a question, as if she were surprised he would remember her like this, the girl in the garden with her smile to the sun.

"I could never forget, Hollie," he managed, glad she couldn't see his face, glad he couldn't look into her eyes as he spoke. "I couldn't forget a thing about you. I tried. Believe me, I tried."

She pulled back slightly, though she didn't break the contact of their fingers, and when Cade opened his eyes, she stood closer to him than he would have thought.

"I never meant to hurt you," she managed, the truth so obvious in those deep blue eyes, and he believed her. But it didn't matter, not now.

"You did hurt me, though," Cade managed. "Hol, you were just about the only person I cared about in this town. And you just left. How…how was I supposed to feel?"

It wasn't anger in his voice, not anymore. He had never been quick to anger and that had been half the problem. For so long, Cade had accepted that life was easier for some people, accepted that he would never have sunny days and cozy nights, accepted it and allowed it and never questioned *why him*. Then Hollie and Wes had moved next door and it had been like a light switch had turned. Ruthie Callihan had opened her doors to so many of the stragglers her wayward grandchildren had collected and Hollie had made him see that life could be so much better, if he allowed himself to ask for more.

No, it wasn't anger. But his throat was scratchy and his heart hurt and he ached to hold her, to pull her into his arms and never let her run away again.

"I..." She hesitated. "I told Sawyer I couldn't tell him why I left without telling you too." Hollie, the woman who jumped, climbed and danced first, was looking at the toe of her boot with rapt fascination and avoiding eye contact. "I can't tell you without telling him too."

Cade dropped her hand and turned away from her, but before he got far, Hollie grabbed his arm. The movement brought them even closer together and it made his heart beat for an entirely different reason now, one that had nothing to do with anger or sadness and everything to do with the primal lust that this woman had inspired in him all those years ago, and continued to inspire within him now.

God, she had grown even more beautiful with the passing of time, with the memories and adventures that sparkled behind those bright blue eyes, with the way her smart mouth had become even smarter and her body more her own, lithe and muscled and full. Cade was *extremely* aware of how full, of how her breasts plumped against her jacket, of how her round, delectable ass filled out a pair of unflattering cargo pants like it was God's own plan.

"I'm not asking for forgiveness," Hollie said, her voice breathy and a soft hint of pink rising up the smooth column of her neck to stain those pretty cheeks.

"I'm just going to say that I made young, foolish decisions. And I regret them." She slid her hand up his arm and brought it to rest on his cheek. Her fingers were somehow at once rough and smooth, slightly calloused around the edges, but beautiful for it. "I regret hurting you, Cade. Not a day goes by when I don't."

"Then why haven't you come back?" he managed, trying oh so hard to focus on this oh-so-important conversation and not the way her simplest touch made him practically animalistic with need. She was touching his *face*, for God's sake, and yet his cock was throbbing in anticipation and pure, unadulterated heat was coursing through his body at her proximity. She was so close, close enough that if he just leaned down, he could take what she was offering up with those full pink lips and finish what they had started all those years ago.

"I was scared," she admitted.

Cade shook his head. "Hollie Callihan doesn't get scared of anything," he murmured. "I've seen you take on black diamond slopes like they're bunny hills."

She didn't even crack a smile. "I was scared," she repeated, as if only just realizing it herself for the first time.

Cade couldn't help himself—he brought his own hand up to caress her cheek this time, fool that he was. The connection was undeniable, the soft heat of her skin making him wonder about all the other soft heat she had to offer.

"And now?" he asked. Hell, was that his voice? It sounded primal and anticipatory and one thread away from the complete unraveling of his hard-earned self-control.

"Terrified," she whispered.

It was the look in her eyes that broke him. Or maybe the way she clenched his shirt with her strong, delicate fingers and pulled him close. Maybe he pulled her close. Cade honestly didn't know, and the moment their mouths met, he didn't give a good goddamn. It was a clash of heat and need, lightning on a rainless night, bursting in sparks and fire all around them, as if it had been building for so very long that there had never been any other option but manic explosion.

He slid his tongue across the seam of her lips and she yielded to him, opening to his exploring kiss and giving him just a taste more, when he needed her in full, had needed her in full for so very long that he thought he might just explode on the spot. He was going to need one hell of a cold shower when he got home.

After a long moment, she pulled back, though she remained in the circle of his arms—when had he wrapped himself so fully around her? Her eyes were hooded and her lips swollen—she looked like a woman interrupted in the midst of a good ravishing, and Cade was firmly of the mind that a good ravishing was not to be interrupted.

"I'm sorry," she said quietly. "I'm not acting myself right now. I shouldn't have done that."

Her apology, her uncertainty, were unsettling. Hollie had never been a woman to second-guess herself, never been a woman to shy away from the unknown or the difficult or the complicated. And yet, she was back here, back among her oldest friends after nearly a decade away from them. Of course it was going to be difficult for her.

"This conversation isn't over," Cade told her quietly and stepped back from her embrace to keep from diving in and kissing her all over again. As desperately as he wanted to feel her against him, against every part of him, it was more important that he knew what the hell had caused her to tuck tail and run all those years ago. And he wasn't going to let her leave without the information — whether Hollie knew it or not.

"I know," she said quietly. "And we will have it. Just not yet." She turned and he followed her around the pathway to the front of the house, stopping only when she pulled up short. She tilted her head and Cade looked over her shoulder to see Cam and Agent Walsh, their heads bent over something on the hood of Hollie's Jeep.

"Unexpected," Hollie murmured, as though her return wasn't unexpected, as though their kiss in the backyard wasn't unexpected, as though his body's reaction to her ass pressed against him wasn't... Actually no, that was entirely expected.

"You trust her?" he asked, a sense of protectiveness and honor kicking in that Cade had obviously misplaced when first finding her here.

"Savannah? Beyond a shadow of a doubt. She's smart as hell and cares for the people in her life. Comes from good stock. Why?"

Cade shook his head. "It's my sworn duty to protect this town," he said, his voice only a little sardonic. "I can't have you federal agents coming in and messing up all of our lives."

Hollie stiffened and Cade knew he should probably make light, should probably take it back, but he couldn't soothe over her wounded feelings every time he expressed how he felt. He might have wanted her, might have ached for her like he'd never wanted another woman in his entire fucking life, but she had hurt him bad and he wasn't ready to put that all in the past.

"Deputy Flores," Hollie said, stepping out from behind the rhododendron that had blocked them from view, "so good to see you again. Glad to see you and Savannah working together so closely."

There was no denying the blush on Savannah Walsh's face. He'd dated a redhead or two in his time and they always blushed, but all Cade could think about was the way the flush had pinked Hollie's cheeks, and how he had been the one to put it there.

Camilla and Savannah stepped too far apart, in the way people did when they felt guilty for something they hadn't done yet. Cade could almost relate.

"Thanks for sharing the emergency routes with me," Savannah said, gathering up the files they had been looking at. "Feel free to call me with any additional information." She climbed into the Jeep and Hollie shot him one last wary glance and nod before she pulled the Jeep back down the dirt road and out of sight.

"So, Savannah Walsh," he said to Camilla, when they climbed into the truck. She raised a dark eyebrow at him.

"So, Hollie Callihan," she said in reply.

So Hollie Callihan, indeed.

Chapter Six

"What can I get you guys?" Maddy Hollis asked the group gathered in the dining room of the Triple Diamond B&B. Across one wall hung a map of the region with several pinpoints and flags highlighting expected emergency areas, and the large table in the center of the room was covered in stacks of folders and files, with no fewer than six cups of coffee between them.

"I think we're okay," Hollie said, standing up straight to stretch. Her back released with an audible *pop*. "Savannah went to grab some pizzas, so why don't you guys stay and eat with us?"

It had been nearly a full week since she had shared a disastrous, decadent kiss with both Sawyer and Cade on the same day—not that she had any intention of telling either of them about the other—and Hollie had been doing her best to ensure she was never alone in the same room as one or both of them. Yes, they deserved an explanation, there was no doubt of that. But she wasn't just a little worried about how they would respond when she finally shared that unseemly truth, and she wasn't about to trust herself alone with either man, not given what had happened the last time.

There was also the whole matter of the daggers she couldn't help but notice them shooting at each other. Cade and Sawyer hadn't exactly been friends, certainly not the way she had been friends with both of them growing up, but there had been nothing to indicate such a potent dislike either. They'd been passing acquaintances, friendly enough, surviving the common, growing-up-poor circumstances each in their own ways—Sawyer with his fists and fury, Cade with his head down and determination sharp.

Hollie, well, she wasn't entirely sure what her coping mechanisms had been, but though they'd lived on the wrong side of town, especially for those oh-so-cruel kids, the sons and daughters of wealthy ranch owners and farmers, she'd had her grandmother and she'd had Wes. Simple dinners and hand-me-down clothes hadn't seemed like a heartache, not with the love she'd had in her life.

But no matter what their relationship had been, the two men—and they were oh-so-deliciously men— seemed to spark with anger and genuine hate when she saw them together. She had noticed it the first day, when striding across the lawn toward the fire engine— bickering, hushed voices, antagonism. And she'd noticed it since, in curt replies, angry expressions, jerky movements. She'd been away so long and so much had changed.

And yet, so much *hadn't*. And that truly was the reason she couldn't be alone with either of these men and far, far more couldn't be alone with both of them. Because she'd run, tail tucked, from Wolf Creek, terrified of the one thing she had been truly afraid of in her life, and those feelings, those desperate imaginings, hadn't gone away with time. In fact, they were stronger now than they had ever been before. She had two prime examples of how those kinds of relationships weren't just fantasy, weren't just the depraved dreams of a stupid, foolish girl.

And God, she wished she didn't.

"I'd love that," Maddy said, settling into the chair beside Hollie. "Christian's working on something out in the field and Ryder is down at the station with Cade, but they'll both be back soon."

Hollie couldn't help the pounding of her heart when Maddy said Cade's name. It was hard to forget the sensation of his body pressed against her own, the way she responded to his touch with animal instinct, how softly and sweetly he had wrapped his fingers into her hand and they had silently traveled down memory lane together.

If only it was that easy.

Because if had just been about Cade, if it had been just about the boy who lived a hundred feet behind her grandmother's house, the boy she'd learned to climb trees with and stayed under a blanket of stars beside until the morning light crept over the Black Reef Mountains, Hollie probably wouldn't have left in the first place—at least, she wouldn't have left alone. But it wasn't just Cade, and the memory of Cade's mouth on her own didn't come alone either, followed harsh and swift by the way Sawyer had tasted—spicy, like cinnamon whisky, rough and demanding in a way that even now, days later, still set her body alight.

"Look who I found," Savannah called, backing into the dining hall with a stack of pizza boxes in her hand.

Camilla Flores followed behind, then the man himself, because why the fuck wouldn't he be here? He glanced at her, and Hollie forced herself to look away from his gaze, from the way those deep brown eyes reminded her of things she was so much better off forgetting.

A ding on her phone was a welcome distraction, until she glanced at the name on the screen.

Headed your way to discuss projection updates. Need anything?

Yeah, to get her head screwed on tight, but there was nothing Hollie could do about that right now.

We're set here. Walsh just grabbed pizza, so double time and you can eat.

She placed the phone face down on the desk and closed her eyes for the briefest moment, letting the world around, the noise and chatter, fade away. She was here for a job, here to do projections and emergency response, a job she had fallen into ass backward and truly loved. She was not here to return to a darkened past that had left her as battered and bruised as the two people she had once cared so much for, the two people she had been trying to protect.

"Is there something between you and the sheriff?" Maddy asked, pulling Hollie from the sweet respite of peace behind her closed eyes. She turned to glance at Maddy, who had folded her legs over the side of her chair and was peering intently up at her. "I'm not from around here, so forgive me for prying. But he's got the wildest expression in his eyes when he looks at you and… I thought I might ask if everything was okay."

Maddy and her sister were good stock. Hollie had decided that from the get-go. Even if they hadn't tamed two of Wolf Creek's most notorious troublemakers and wrangled true love out of her old friends respectively, she would have believed that. They looked out for the people in their lives and genuinely cared about the answer to the question *are you okay?*

Where to begin?

"It's complicated," Hollie said simply. "I haven't been back here in Wolf Creek in a long time."

"Well, I'm an expert at running away from my problems," Maddy said with a wink. "Want a stranger's advice on anything?"

Hollie grinned. "Lily already offered," she said. "And I'm not about to traipse off after two men — not that there's any judgment. But I'm here to do a job."

Maddy raised a shapely eyebrow and glanced over Hollie's shoulder. "Are you sure they know that?" she asked. "Because Fire Captain Matthews looks about ready to shoot daggers."

Hollie swung around in her chair so fast she nearly fell out of it, but she still couldn't ignore the soft chuckles from Maddy's direction.

"Those boys have been at each other's throats since the day I arrived in Wolf Creek," she said. "Ryder and Christian said it's been a lot longer than that."

Hollie managed to tear her gaze away from the sight of Sawyer in a black and red flannel jacket that, coupled with the long red beard and hair and the fierce wildness in his eyes, made him look like some mountain lumberjack returned to civilization.

"How long?" she asked, a sneaking suspicion climbing up her back with the soothing sensation of a tarantula crossing her skin. Maddy just shrugged.

"They didn't say exactly. I think Ryder mentioned that something happened a while back to make 'em dislike each other so much. He says he barely remembers them talking when they were in high school, but Ryder and Christian are a bit older, so what would they even know, right?"

"Right." The bite of pizza Hollie had just taken tasted a little like ash, but there wasn't much she could do about it right now. Two Hollis sisters, four Hollis sisters' — lovers? Partners? Boyfriends? — Savannah, Camilla Flores and two guys from the fire station were spread out around the room and chatting wildly. There was no way she could have this all-important conversation with an audience. Even an audience who would probably understand better than anyone else ever would.

So not the point.

The point was — she was going to have to talk to them. And she was going to have to do it tonight. Together. She hadn't actually planned to tell either of them the truth, not when Sawyer had asked for an explanation, nor when Cade had made it clear he wanted one. She'd been stalling, terrified, unsure. Now, she was all those things — and also determined to set matters straight, no matter how painful it was.

As if on cue, a crack of lightning burst outside the window, followed by the ominous rumbling of thunder not so far in the distance. *Yeah, seems about right.*

Hollie chatted with Maddy and her husbands — husbands! — for a few more minutes about the effects of flash flooding on agriculture and the expected yield for their crops this early in the season. Christian Harlow was covered in ink and wearing a loose Jack Daniel's tank top that showed a hint of curving, powerful muscle from behind a leather jacket. He hardly seemed the type to grow animated over the return on legumes, but his eyes actually did sparkle when discussing the year's crop rotation.

Lily joined them and soon the whole room was engaged in a round table of stories and conversations that started up and left off, finished and repeated. It reminded her of the early years, living with grandma and Wes, back when it had been the three of them, three orphans in their own ways, against the world.

Traveling had been fundamental to her as a person — the next adventure, the next jump, the next climb, the next rescue mission or new destination. They had all helped to make Hollie into who she was. But they had also prevented her from making those lasting connections, from having a dinner table she could return to after late nights, from banter forged after years of love and care and shared experiences.

And I've missed it.

Damn, if that wasn't a dangerous thing to admit, especially when two of the men who had both spent so many nights at her dinner table were *just over there* and she didn't know which eyes were more dangerous to catch, which mouth was curved into a more enticing and troublesome smirk, which strong fingers across folded arms or laid flat on the table were calling to her baser instincts with more misplaced lust.

The room slowly began to empty of people. Lily gave her a long hug and Dec and Micah both stopped by to bid their goodnights. Their Search and Rescue camp just up the mountain from the Triple Diamond Ranch would prove indispensable if predictions surrounding the flood runoffs came to fruition.

"Can we get you guys anything else for the night?" Maddy asked. She, Ryder and Christian began gathering the trash from dinner. "Looks like you'll be burning the midnight oil for a while." She indicated the stack of papers that Hollie had placed on the table behind her.

Hollie smiled. "I think we're okay. I have a few more emergency preparations I'd like to go over, but we can all see to ourselves. You guys have been great, truly." Maddy had a lovely smile and she bestowed it upon Hollie now, before handing a stack of pizza boxes to Christian.

"You're lucky you have a great ass," Hollie heard him murmur, but the expression on his face showed that he had no problem at all with spending his life working by her side. Ryder didn't even try to hide his love for Maddy Hollis, not as he bid them all goodnight, wrapped his arm around her waist and headed out into the fresh spring air.

"It's going to rain," Hollie said, when the door shut behind them, partially because it *was* going to rain — the sky had been cracking with distant lightning and the wind was thick with moisture — and partially because she wasn't sure what to say next. Savannah and Camilla were still in the room with them and no part of Hollie want to ask them to leave. She did actually have work to go over with all of them and the conversation she would eventually have to share with Sawyer and Cade had no promises of being an easy one.

"Fits our climate models," Savannah put in. "If the storms start today, we can expect the dams to reach capacity within forty-eight hours."

The small group of them had gathered at the end of the long table, and even in her state of constant awareness of the two men in the room, Hollie couldn't deny that Savannah was sitting closer to Camilla Flores than was strictly necessary.

Good for her. We don't all have to give up dreams of love and acceptance.

"Sav's right." Hollie stood from the table and walked over the map of Lewis and Clark County. "The Wolf Creek Bridge is priority, since we're going to need a quick evacuation route if it comes to that. Cade, I want you to take point on bridge management." She turned to face him, which was a mistake. He had taken off his regulation jacket on first arriving, but Hollie hadn't allowed herself to enjoy the way his dark green Henley pulled across those muscles, muscles she had felt under her fingertips, muscles that she wanted to taste, to touch to caress from when she had first understood what if meant to feel those things. This Cade was not a young man still in his early adulthood. He was pure and masculine and full of strength, and she couldn't deny how much it called to her, how much she wanted to do more than stand in her backyard and hold hands.

This isn't about that, Hollie.

It wasn't. Of course it wasn't. But her fears about coming home hadn't been entirely due to the conversation she was going to have tonight, the one where she'd be forced to explain so many things she didn't fully understand herself. No, so much of that fear, so much of what had kept her away for nearly a decade was thanks to this need, this terrifying want that struck her sideways every time she so much as glanced Cade's way.

And Sawyer's.

Fuck.

"Sawyer." She turned from Cade's face and that was nearly her undoing. For as relaxed as Cade looked out of his regulation sheriff's jacket, his hair as mussed as it could be at the near military length, Sawyer had gone full bad boy. He was leaning back in his chair, feet crossed at the ankles, hands behind his head and an expression on his face that Hollie would dream about in the darkest hours of the night. The ink adorning his wrists and forearms moved with his gentle rocking and she had to swallow hard to keep from making some very rash decisions. "Sawyer, we need you on tree duty. We're concerned about power outages and damages from both whatever the storm brings down and whatever the water runoff adds to. We may actually see some of that tonight."

She turned toward the window and peeked outside, partially because it was her job to get a read on the weather and update her records with every change, and partially because the expression in Sawyer's eyes had been temptation incarnate, dangerous and sinful and just as hot at Cade's demanding gaze. No, she'd never been the type do anything by half, but this was ridiculous.

"Sure you can handle that, Matthews?" Cade asked, his deep voice pulling at something inside her. "Should we get some tinsel for all your tree trimming?"

Camilla looked bored and Sawyer only raised an eyebrow, like a centurion rounding his opponent, preparing for a showdown.

"While I'm at the store, I can pick up some flotation devices for you, just in case the water goes past your ankles," he replied.

"Guys," Hollie cut in. She liked a good bit of ribbing now and again and she knew all too well that both men were capable of being carefree and fun, but these barbs weren't. They were laden with something she didn't like and it was coming time to figure out what the fuck was going on between them.

"What do you want us to do about the East Reservoir?" Camilla asked, because thank God for women who had good heads on their shoulders. "Should we be worried about contamination?"

Hollie glanced back up at the map. The reservoir was about twenty miles away and could either be hit hard or entirely unscathed in the melee.

"I could go down and take a look, boss," Savannah said, grabbing the map in front of her. "Rain's not due to start for at least an hour or so."

Hollie chewed her lip. She should let Savannah go, even though it was past dark and she wasn't loving the idea of sending her closest friend out into the storm, whenever it was set to start.

"I'll go with her," Camilla volunteered. "My house is out that way, so we have a place to bunk if the storm comes early." Hollie definitely didn't miss the flush that spread across Savannah's face, and that was all it took to convince her. Just because Hollie wasn't keen on the conversation that was about to take place didn't mean she couldn't give Savannah a choice. And she really did need more info on the angle and proximity of the reservoir entrance to where their runoff was expected.

"Fine," Hollie said. She picked a handful of forms out of one folder and placed them down on the table before Savannah. "These are the numbers we really need," she said, indicating with her pen and circling a few of the relevant sections. Savannah nodded and slid the pages into her plastic clipboard.

"Grab your parka — chances are good you're going to get wet."

Savannah, who had been taking a sip from her bottle of water, coughed hard and Hollie had to fight to hold back a laugh. She hadn't meant to embarrass her friend, really, but some things were too good to pass up.

"In all seriousness," she said, her voice taking on the tone of a woman with first-hand experience of emergency situations that hadn't been managed properly, "if the storm gets too bad tonight, I don't want you out there. Get to the sheriff deputy's house and hole up. And call me. It's not worth getting injured over."

Savannah nodded, and with one more handshake from Flores, the red-faced farm girl and the sheriff deputy beat a hasty retreat.

Leaving Hollie alone in the room with Sawyer Matthews and Cade Easton, the two men she had dreamed about, had thought about in her weak moments, had nearly come back to visit so very many times. She owed them so much more than an explanation, but how could she even offer that when she didn't exactly have one herself?

"Okay, so if we follow protocol X6, that should be on pages ten through twelve…"

"Cut the shit, Hol," Sawyer said. His words were rough but his tone was surprisingly soft. Even a tough guy like Sawyer wasn't immune to good old-fashioned hurt feelings. "You've been avoiding me and I'm going to out on a limb and guess that you've been avoiding Easton too. We've read the protocols and we know what we're up against." He sat forward and put his elbows on the table in a display of masculine power that should *not* have caught her attention. "What we don't know is what the fuck made you run away with your tail between your legs and never look back."

Hollie closed her eyes, but she could hear Cade stand from his chair to lean against the table. When she opened them again, his arms were folded and he cut a large, impressive figure, all shoulders and muscles and a hell of a dangerous expression in his eyes.

"I may not agree with Matthews on much," he said. "But I do agree with him on this. What happened, Hollie? Why'd you leave all this behind?" She heard his unspoken words — *why did you leave* us *behind?*

Because I was scared. Because I didn't understand how I could feel so strongly for two people at once. Because I couldn't stay if I hurt either of you, so I hurt you both instead and myself in the process.

"Why don't we start with something simpler?" she asked. Was it her imagination, or was the storm outside starting to pick up? Surely that was the sound of rain beginning to patter against the roof of the dining hall and not her own heart threatening to escape.

Mount Manadonak. Mount Whitney. Mount Temple.

Child's play, compared with the uphill journey she had ahead of her right now.

"Why are you guys acting like you haven't known each other for nearly thirty years? I know you weren't exactly close before…before. But you seem to really hate each other."

The expression exchanged between Sawyer and Cade couldn't exactly be described as hate. It was more the unhappy mutual allyship of two people who knew something she didn't know, and Hollie didn't like the sensation one bit. Hence she jumped nearly a foot in the air when the crack of thunder above their heads shook the glass around them.

For want of something to do, Hollie added a handful of logs to the dwindling fire, even though it was more than plenty warm in the dining hall and seemed to be getting hotter by the second.

"You really don't get it, do you, Hol?" Sawyer asked. The nickname, not for the first time, made her heart feel small. She and Savannah were close, closer with every trip they took together, and she worked with many capable people, stayed in decent touch with friends from her travels around the world, folks like Dec and Micah she had known in the midst of emergency and chaos. But with Grandma long gone and Wes in small villages with far bigger fish to fry, she had few people to call her by familiar, intimate nicknames and it...

Does not make me sad, thank you very much.

"What's there to get?" she asked, acknowledging that she could stall no longer. She moved back toward the table and placed her hands flat, arms out, as if the simple defensive pose was enough to keep a decade of demons away.

"We didn't know why you left," Cade put in. "Hell, we still have no idea. Hard not to blame the people still around." His tone was so matter of fact that it took a moment for Hollie to even register what he had meant. Her jaw dropped.

"You've been fighting with each other for ten years because of me?" She sagged against the table and rubbed her hands over her face. "Fuck... *Fuck*. I never meant for any of this to happen." When she opened her eyes, she made eye contact first with Cade, then with Sawyer. "I know you guys have never been close, but I'm not worth fighting over. Not like this."

Cade stepped forward and she couldn't have ignored the power of his presence if her life had depended on it. He might have looked the prim and proper lawman on the outside, but there was a heady darkness in his eyes that called to something baser within her. She wanted to feel it, wanted to open the mystery of who he was and what made him tick, and she wanted to do it right now.

"That's where you're wrong, Hol," he murmured, and God, he was so close now she could feel his breath against her neck, the scent of fresh mountain air on his skin, mired in coffee and Cade. "You've always been worth fighting for."

Chapter Seven

She felt Sawyer behind her before they even touched, her body just as attuned to his presence as it was to Cade's, though for entirely different reasons. They were like fire and water, each capable of their own brand of destruction, beauty and chaos, together, a force of wills that turned out differently every time.

"Can't let you have all the fun, Easton," Sawyer said, though the words were without a doubt directed at her. "Why don't we give Hollie the choice to do with us as she pleases?" He damn near purred the word *pleases* and Hollie's ability to form a coherent sentence was disappearing by the second. They were both so big and masculine and capable and she ached for touches she knew wouldn't come. There was no doubt in her mind this was a punishment for leaving, and one she deserved, no matter how much it made her want the impossible.

"That's...not fair." Not the right choice of words, but the proximity of so much masculinity was undoubtedly shorting out her normally capable brain. "I care for you both, I always have." Understatement of the century, but how on earth could she articulate what she really meant when Cade's thigh was pressing against her own and Sawyer's strong fingers were brushing her knuckles with such smoothness and promise that she could probably find her release from that alone?

"But you didn't trust us," Cade murmured. "Either of us, Hollie. You never asked. You just left. And it's time for an explanation."

The storm outside was raging in earnest now, lightning cracking against a black sky, rolls of thick, weighty thunder overhead, the pounding of her heart in her chest and the heat between her legs, all in tandem with the chaos of nature.

"I wanted you both that night," she said. Half-truth, but at least she had managed it. "That night down by the lake, after graduation. I wanted you both. And it scared me."

Scared her enough to send the woman who had skydived on her eighteenth birthday and subsequently traveled the world to mountain climb, scuba dive and perform search and rescue missions, to leave in the dead of night without a word. Because she was far from telling them everything, and 'everything' was an insurmountable climb.

"Obviously," Sawyer said. He was close enough to her now that his beard brushed against her neck, and the sensation made her shiver.

"Obviously?" she managed. Was that her voice? It was difficult to tell, high as it was.

"Obviously," Cade repeated. "But you didn't give us the chance to find that out, did you, Hol? You went home. We thought we'd never see you again. And, naturally, we blamed each other." He shot a dark look at Sawyer over the top of her head and Hollie took the opportunity to grasp for an equilibrium that would not come. "Still do, in fact."

One major complication to deal with at a time.

"Wouldn't you have been scared in the same situation?" she asked. "What would you have done if you were me? Stuck around to get rejected and have your heart broken or leave for a new life?"

Sawyer placed his hand under her chin and turned her head to face him. His dark green eyes were positively ablaze and Hollie's breath caught.

"You could have trusted us," he whispered. "We may not have been best friends, Hol, but we were both your best friend and you could have trusted us."

To her surprise, he glanced over to Cade as if seeking his agreement. Even more amazingly, Cade gave a short nod, as if their years of bickering could be placed aside for this conversation, a conversation where she spoke aloud and they communicated in micro-expressions only men understood.

Before she could think further on it, a flash of lightning cut hard across the sky and all the lights in the dining hall went out, sending the room into semi-darkness. Hollie closed her eyes against the intimacy of the firelight and the soft shadows and the nearness of these two men with as many secrets as her own. Removing one sense only improved her other ones and she was keenly aware of the way Sawyer smelled, like fresh lumber and warm flannel and whiskey, aware of the heat of Cade's muscled thigh against her own, aware of the intensity of their anticipation as if it were in neon fucking lights against the night sky.

"I did trust you," she managed, so quietly she was surprised she could be heard over the storm. "It was myself I didn't trust. Because when I think—"

Cade cut her off. "Do you trust us now, Hol?" he asked, not giving her the chance to walk back off the precipice. He slid his hand up her leg and that simple touch pulled Hollie's brain far away from the conversation at hand, in a direction that should have terrified her. But, naturally, it didn't.

"Of course," she managed, her tone base and demanding with those simple words.

"Then don't think," he said quietly, and she realized that in the dark he had moved close, closer still, and he brought his lips down on her own with an intensity as strong as the storm raging outside. Hollie couldn't help herself—she kissed him back just as intensely, all the while dragging her nails up Sawyer's forearm, corded with muscle and power that made her ache.

I wanted you both.

Obviously.

Of course, they had to both know how this was going to end, since apparently, the entire world had known back then, and Hollie wasn't strong enough to fight it— not now, not with the way Sawyer's mouth felt against her throat. He trailed hot, delicious kisses along the nape of her neck that practically burned her skin. At the same time, Cade's tongue pressed against her lips and she yielded so easily to his exploration and promise. After a moment, she pulled back slightly from Cade's kiss, her lips swollen and her breath coming in short, desperate pants. She found Sawyer's face and dragged him in for a kiss, and Cade took over pressing his mouth to her neck.

"What are we doing?" she asked, leaning back from Sawyer, finally finding some sense of herself in the overwhelming onslaught of pleasure and need.

"I would have thought that was obvious," Cade murmured, his mouth still hot against her skin. "But apparently some of us have to work harder if we're going to get the message across."

"I can give you some tips, if you'd like," Sawyer replied without missing a beat. Hollie felt as though she were wading through molasses.

"I know what we're *doing*," she said, lacking every ounce of authoritative control she had learned at Debra Lewitt's side over the last five years. "What I mean is, what the hell are we doing?"

"Showing you what you missed out on, Hollyhock," Sawyer growled, his need doing something to her own she didn't understand. "Giving you a taste of what you could have had."

Deep down, in the part of her heart she had long locked up, Hollie knew as an irrefutable truth that a taste of these two men wasn't going to be enough, not for a single night and not for the years of lonely ones that hovered ahead. But she had been fighting her instincts on this, fighting the carnal need that had driven her to utter distraction, for far, far too long, and there was no resistance left, not against their heat or their promise or the way they made her feel.

"This is crazy." Her mind was muddled and her breath was getting caught in her chest. "You guys don't even like each other."

"True," Sawyer mused. "But we both like you. And unless you're planning to kick one of us out, I think we're both willing to take what you're willing to give."

"Agreed." Cade's voice was already rough and the sound of it had Hollie clamping her thighs together instinctually.

We both like you.

She *wasn't* willing to kick either of them out. If this was going to happen, and she had all the proof in the world that it was *going to happen*, it had to be with both of them. It was the only way.

"We need rules." Her words came out on a choked breath, and she could barely hear them over the drumming of her heart in her ears.

"Don't run off again," Cade whispered in her ear. His breath was hot against her skin and the sensation made her writhe, made her body want more, something she couldn't have.

"No chance," she replied, allowing her head to fall back so that two masculine, powerful forces could descend on her needy body at once.

This is madness.

Without a doubt, it was. But her breasts were tingling with need and her nipples had pebbled to hard, almost painful points behind her tank top. The heat between her legs was spreading, up her spine, her neck, making her face flush and her eyes close.

"Promise that you'll talk to us," Sawyer muttered against her skin. God, but the feeling of his beard, rough and thick, made her ache for the sensation between her legs. "After. Promise we'll talk." If she had half a mind present that wasn't focusing on the way they two men played her body like a fiddle, she would find it interesting that Sawyer Matthews, inked-up daredevil with a chip on his shoulder, was the one who wanted to talk. But she didn't have the presence of mind for anything so deep and she simply nodded.

"Promise, Hollie," Cade added. He stopped kissing her neck and Sawyer stopped moving his fingers below the hem of her shirt at the same moment, and Hollie sighed, though the sound came out petulant and needy.

In the firelight, Sawyer raised one thick eyebrow, and he brought his hand to her mouth to rub his thumb across her swollen lower lip.

"Brat," he murmured. "I look forward to teaching you a lesson. Starting with taking direction properly, Hollyhock. If you want more, you're going to have do as you're told."

Hollie hadn't exactly been celibate in her years away from Montana and all the secrets it held. She'd indulged in her fair share of adventurous sex, the kind that fit the way she lived her life. An experience or several in a specific club in downtown Denver had taught her that being told what to do was something that worked two hundred percent of the time, but nothing had prepared her for the controlled, measured command in Sawyer's voice, or the rough hold of Cade's hand wrapping her wrists together behind her back.

"I promise," she managed, her voice husky and unfamiliar. "Now, God, please someone touch me."

Neither of them moved.

"You want to be fucked on the table?" Sawyer asked. "Right in front of the window, spread out and displayed for the world to see?" It went without saying that not a soul without a death wish was outside in the current storm, but Hollie felt the weight of those words regardless.

"Yes," she managed. "On the table. Both of you."

Both of you.

As if she hadn't been dreaming of this moment, this fantasy for years. As if the table, the couch, the bed, the floor, hell, her backyard, hadn't factored in the way these two men had taken her. She'd fantasized about them on their own too, but those specific lonely nights, the ones where she gave herself over to the truly depraved desires, had looked a hell of a lot like this.

Sawyer pressed his finger into her mouth and she yielded to him without question, sucking him deep and not bothering to hide the groan that escaped her lips at the sensation. She wanted so much more, but she had no doubt that Cade and Sawyer would play by their own rules, ones that would undoubtedly turn her entire body into rubber by the end of the night.

"What do you think, Easton?" Sawyer asked. "Should we give the lady what she wants?"

It was the first time she'd heard Sawyer ask Cade a question without a bite to his tone, and her heart swelled at the idea that they could come together — for her.

But Cade shook his head, and God, for playing the good-boy role so fucking well, that man could smirk like a pirate captain before a raid. His dark eyes were lidded and the smile on his face promised pleasure like she'd never known before. From their kiss earlier in the week, Hollie already knew, could already guess what their coming together would be like, how it would push her body to the very limits.

"She's not desperate enough yet," he said to Sawyer, though he was looking directly at her. "Gonna make you scream my name tonight, Hollie. And you're gonna love every fucking second of it."

"Right up until she screams my name louder," Sawyer replied, and though she wasn't looking at him, she could hear the arrogant smirk in his voice too.

"If someone doesn't fucking touch me, I swear to God, I'll do it myself," Hollie muttered. She kicked her shoes off and pulled her sweatshirt over her head to toss it somewhere to the side. She pulled the ponytail down too until her hair curled over her bare shoulders, then started on her pants.

"That's quite enough of that," Sawyer muttered. He pushed her back on the table and began the slow work of unbuttoning and unzipping her jeans. He made a point of brushing over her skin with every inch of denim he pushed down and Hollie tried to arch into his touch until Cade's strong hand pressed down into her hip.

"Let us take care of you, Hollie," he said. "Trust us. Or at least trust me and let Sawyer figure it out…" His tone was teasing, though, with none of the menace he normally used to speak with Sawyer. But then he moved one hand to the strap of her tank top and pulled it down, exposing the light blue lace bra below, and she wasn't thinking too much about the inexplicable male ego, except in regard to how it made her feel. She didn't afford herself too many luxuries out in the field — her shirts were regulation, her boots meant for work and not design, but she loved a nice set of lingerie.

Judging by the dark groan that had just come from Cade's throat, so did he.

"I never thought I'd be grateful for a government windbreaker," he muttered. "But if I knew you were walking around wearing this every day, I wouldn't be able to concentrate on anything."

"It's a match set," Sawyer growled, when he pulled her jeans free and tossed them to the side. She felt exposed and desired, half on the conference table in her lingerie, loose hair spilled across her breasts.

"Fuck, you're so pretty," he added. He positioned himself between her legs and slid down to his knees. Cade brought one hand up to her breast and slowly began to tease the swollen flesh. She needed more – her body was already right at the edge of control and resistance and they were tempting her slowly, kisses to the inside of her thigh, not-enough touches across her swollen nipples. Cade brushed her with the tip of his thumb and she hissed at the contact.

"More." Honestly, the only word she could come up with right now. He wasted no time. He leaned over the table and took her lace-clad nipple into his mouth, brushing it gently with his teeth.

"Bite me, fuck, Cade, please…" It was garbled and mumbled, but she seemed to get the meaning across just fine because he pressed his teeth into her swollen flesh, the hum of pain and pleasure a beautiful riptide across her entire body. He bit harder this time and the need between her legs increased, slick heat building up her spine.

"You like a little a pain with your pleasure," he muttered. "That can be arranged." He wrapped his hand in her hair and pulled her up to meet his kiss, all the while massaging her swollen breasts. Her mind was so wrapped around the way he felt against her mouth that she nearly lost it when Sawyer pressed his lips to her wet panties.

The sensation was overwhelming and not nearly enough at the same time. His thick beard tickled the inside of her legs, made her ache for more texture, more touch, something that would help her ride the mounting pressure.

"You're so fucking wet," he growled against her pussy, the words sending vibrations through her body that made Hollie arch up in need and frustration. "Gonna be so fucking slick sliding into you." He stroked her with his fingers and tongue, the sensation of lace against her entrance delicious but not enough. None of it seemed to be enough as the two men coaxed her to orgasm with sinful promises and rough touches. She wrapped her hand in Sawyer's hair and pressed him into her body, enjoying the soft chuckle he made against her skin.

"You're looking for a little punishment, aren't you?" Cade asked, and somehow that Dom voice was a natural part of him, seamless and fitting, as if telling aroused women what to do was part of who he was. Hollie had no complaints.

"You wouldn't dare," she moaned, trying to push him, trying to make him carry out the unspoken threat left in the air.

"It would be my pleasure to punish you, sweet one," he murmured. "The very idea of turning your pretty ass red is enough to make my cock leak. And I wouldn't even let you taste it because I know that's what you want."

She couldn't deny that. The idea of taking Cade in her mouth while Sawyer took her body from behind had shivers of untethered pleasure shooting up her spine.

"Please," she managed, though God only knew what she was begging for.

"Please punish you or please let you suck my cock?" he asked. "I don't know if you've earned it yet, princess."

"Keep talking to her like that," Sawyer growled. "She's so wet." He slid his tongue across the entrance to her pussy with a slow, deliberate movement that made Hollie buck wildly, despite the two sets of powerful hands holding her in place.

"Is that what you want, darlin'?" Cade teased, his finger barely tracing the curve of her breast, so lightly it was driving her mad, combined with the assault of Sawyer's tongue on her heat, enough to make her combust with just a little bit more…

Please.

"Tell me, Hollie," Cade continued, as if he had all the self-control in the word. *Fucker probably does.* "Do you like being told what to do? Do you like being spread out on the table for us to touch and taste? Do you like taking orders?" Sawyer slowed his relentless motion against her pussy and she strained to get more contact.

"Answer him, Hollie," he said, standing to position his body between her sprawled legs. "Tell us what you want and you'll get it."

Her mind was going to mush, but Hollie could come up with the important information despite the haze of sensations wracking her body.

"Yes," she said, moaning at the sensation of Cade's fingers against one breast and Sawyer's cock throbbing against the inside of her leg from behind his jeans.

"Yes, what, princess?" Sawyer demanded. "I know you have filthy, dirty thoughts in that brilliant brain of yours and I want to hear every last one."

"Yes, I like being told what to do," she managed. Her release was so close, if only someone would just *touch* her. "Yes, I like getting fucked at both ends, Jesus Christ, yes, I like getting punished."

"You're getting punished right now," Cade whispered to her. "Do you like it?"

Hollie could only let out a desperate groan. Her body was rioting with need and one touch would be enough to send her right over the edge.

"Please," she managed. "Sir."

In the darkness, Cade's gaze flicked to Sawyer's then Sawyer sank back between her thighs and pressed his mouth to her at the same moment as he slid one finger under her lace panties and inside her needy hole.

Hollie screamed. She bucked against him once, twice, once more, and the world fell out from under her and she broke apart in a cataclysm of need and pleasure and aching want. Sparks of light danced at the corners of her closed eyes and her body trembled with her release. She rode the cresting waves until the intensity began to recede and she finally opened her eyes. Sawyer and Cade were both standing before her, their expressions equally potent, but so incredibly different. Sawyer looked almost carnal, as if he were ready to throw her over his shoulder and carry her to bed. Cade had the intense look she had seen in her club countless times, a man holding on to his control, but so capable of causing a storm when he let it go.

"Hollie." Sawyer was the first to speak. It made sense, in an odd sort of way—since her brain had most definitely not put itself back to rights after all the mind-boggling pleasure. But he was the gentle giant of the two, strong and powerful and never afraid to back down from a fight, but the man would play Santa Claus at church without being asked twice. *Firefighters.*

Hmm, I never thought I'd have a Christmas fetish...

"Talk later," she murmured, her voice husky from the moaning they had so easily pulled from her. "We have unfinished business."

Chapter Eight

Without waiting for either of them, she slid off the table and walked over to the rug before the fire. It was soft and cozy and far more comfortable than the chilly conference table had been. Not to mention, she was going to have a hard enough time coming to work without thinking about...well, coming, actually. *Best move the fun away from the real reason I'm here in Wolf Creek.* Which she was not going to think about right now.

"Now, do I have to start by myself or are we going to turn this into a party?" She was nervous. It wasn't like her to ramble, but now that the maddening pleasure they had plied her with was beginning to subside, it was difficult not to be overwhelmed by all the reasons this was a remarkably terrible idea, despite how very much she still wanted it.

"Honey, a man would have to be dead or gay not to want you," Cade said, his smile dipping into that dangerous smirk, and he practically swaggered over to where she stood, Sawyer hot on his heels. "I think we're going to take our time with you, what do you think, Matthews?"

They were standing before her, appraising her mostly naked body, and Hollie couldn't help the thrill of raw satisfaction she felt at their dark gazes. Matters were far from settled between the two men and even further from settled where she was concerned, but if they were willing to put aside past disagreements to make her feel like *that* all over again, she certainly wasn't going to be the dumb woman who stopped them.

"Mmm, she is sweet," Sawyer said to Cade. "I can't wait to feel her."

It shouldn't have turned her on, this sense of being talked about like she wasn't even in the room, these dark and dirty promises. But Hollie had long ago learned to embrace the wild and exciting things that made her feel alive, inside the bedroom and out, and she only wanted more.

"Then what are you waiting for?" she asked. She came to stand between the two men, pressing her back into Sawyer and grinding against him. She began the slow unbuttoning of Cade's shirt. He wore a plain white T-shirt below his button-down and part of Hollie wanted to say 'fuck it' and rip the damn thing in two, but a far larger part of her wanted to tease the two men the way they had teased her, taking her right to the brink and not quite pushing until they nearly lost their minds.

Sawyer seemed to be halfway there already, if the straining erection pressing against her ass was any indication. God, he felt large and hot and Hollie ached for him, for something to curb the sense of emptiness and need that had her returning his harsh touch despite having just found her pleasure a moment ago. The only signs that Cade was starting to lose his cool were the darkening expression in his deep brown eyes and the guttural groan that tore from his throat when she slid her fingers below the band of his pants to pull his shirt free. She might have been putty in these men's hands, but she did know a thing or two about seduction and turn-about was most definitely fair play.

Sawyer pressed a kissed to the back of her neck, but she wasn't about to cede control to him, not again. So she slid Cade's shirt from his strong shoulders and pushed it off and onto the floor, then turned to face Sawyer, whose expression was rich with heat that made Hollie want to give up on the whole charade just to take him right then and there.

We're getting to that.

Still, her fingers were far less steady when she pushed his Henley up his tight, muscled chest and, with Sawyer's help, over his broad shoulders, then his head. He tossed the shirt aside and she brought her hand up to smooth his loose red waves out of his eyes. His gaze was burning her though now, making her pussy ache and pulse, and Hollie didn't have it in herself to wait. She pulled his hair hard and dragged Sawyer's lips to meet her own.

All hell broke loose. She heard Cade kick off his shoes behind her. Then he was kissing along her back and running his hands up and down her arms at the same time. Sawyer pressed her against Cade's front, all the while kissing her with the force of the storm outside. He brought one of his strong hands to her bra and quickly unfastened it, helping her free of the straps and throwing it to the floor.

"Fuck, you're beautiful," he growled, before leaning down to take one straining nipple in his mouth. He bit down slightly on the hardened flesh and Hollie leaned back against Cade's hard chest for support when her legs began to give way, wrapping her arms around his neck to pull him down for another smoldering, potent kiss. She reached for Cade's belt and she fumbled with it, pulling it free with the kind of *snap* that brought to mind nights similar to this one. Only nothing was similar to this, not like this, with the two men she had once cared about most in the world showing her pleasure like she'd never truly known with just their fingers and mouths.

Then Sawyer's mouth was moving lower and he was pulling her lace panties off his with his teeth before sliding them down her legs. She kicked them off and nearly squealed when his large hand came to cup the swollen flesh of her cunt, dripping and slick and so, so empty. Sawyer didn't wait, simply slid a thick finger into her heat, and Hollie nearly screamed at the contact and relief. She arched back into Cade when Sawyer added a second finger, moving them slowly in and out of her body until Hollie was moving wildly against him.

"Don't come," Sawyer demanded. "If you come, you don't get any more."

"I don't think she can do it," Cade stated, matter-of-factly, as if Hollie wasn't squirming wildly in his arms. "I think just hearing us talking makes her want to come. Right, Hollyhock?" He turned to her. "If I so much as tell you that I'm going to fuck your sweet, pretty mouth while Sawyer takes you from behind, you'll cream all over his hands, won't you?"

"I have more self-control than you might think," she managed, though the effect was mostly lost to the husky tone of her voice and the way she writhed helplessly against Sawyer's hands.

"You do not," Sawyer whispered, bringing his mouth to her other ear so Hollie was entirely and completely boxed in by these strong, beautiful men playing her body like a goddamn harp. "You jump first and never ask questions. You're fearless and brilliant and impulsive and you go after what you want."

Despite the haze of pleasure surrounding her, Hollie was reminded that these men *knew* her, deeply, far more intimately than a single night of pleasure. They knew what she had dreamed of, what she had feared. They had seen her soul, and though nearly a decade had passed, she couldn't help but think they still could.

"Mmm, and what do I want right now?" she asked, riding them both at the same time, two swollen, throbbing cocks behind taut pants pressing against her body and keeping her trapped — as if she would ever try to escape from this.

"You want to be filled," Cade said, wrapping one arm around to roughly caress her peaked nipple. "You want to be fucked hard and fast and rough. You want to jump over that edge of control and never look back." He pinched her swollen flesh hard and she gasped and bucked against Sawyer's rough hands. "But you're not going to get that. You're going to get controlled. You're going to get patience. And you're going to get everything you've ever wanted. On our terms."

Our terms.

If only this truce could last.

He leaned down and trailed his teeth over the curve of her shoulder, nipping heated flesh, each pulse of pain like electricity through her body and mind, beautiful, brilliant, overwhelming, calling to her baser instincts.

"Now, be a good girl and suck Sawyer's cock."

Hollie groaned at the words, because she was weak, desperate, needy when it came to being told what to do, and right now she wanted nothing so much as his fat, thick cock in her mouth. Well, maybe Cade's in her swollen cunt, but she was following his rules and doing it his way, and if that meant sliding down to her knees, she wasn't going to complain.

They made just enough space for her to kneel before him and Sawyer began the slow, tormenting motions of removing his belt, then undoing his buttons, batting away her hands when she tried to tug on the zipper. He kicked off his socks and boots and stepped out of his jeans with slow, deliberate movements, his dark gaze never leaving hers. Then he stood before her in navy boxer briefs that did nothing to hide the swell of his thick cock.

For me. He wants me.

The thought was heady and insane and it made Hollie's entire body tingle in anticipation.

"You're so pretty kneeling before my cock," he muttered, bringing his thumb to her lip and swiping it across her swollen flesh. Hollie sucked him into her mouth and he groaned, but his grin only grew wider and more devilish, a testament to the way their encounter was impacting him, wild and mad, just as it made her.

"You should see yourself right now, princess," he whispered. "You're like a feast spread out for the taking. And I am so hungry."

"Ask him for permission, honey," Cade demanded. "Use your words."

Twin groans echoed through the room. Hollie wasn't certain when Cade had become their master of ceremonies, but the role was so right and he was so perfectly attuned to everything she needed to give and take that she had no right to complain.

"Please, Sawyer," she managed. She knew how she must look, all swollen and ravished beyond anything she had ever felt before. She didn't care.

"Please what, princess?" he demanded, his smirk and humor gone, only desperation and need watching her, promising her…

"Please…please can I suck your cock?" The words came out choked and needy, but fuck if they didn't make her wet as hell, begging for the chance to lick him and bring him pleasure. She ached for it and wasn't planning on waiting around much longer.

Cade wrapped his hand in her hair and, with a rough tug that was just short of painful, tilted her head back to look him in the eye.

"Try again, Hollie," he said. "Make it seem like you really want it." She didn't just want it. She wanted the chance to prove herself, to make these two men understand that she had always cared for them, that it had always been her and them against the world.

"I want to choke on your cock," she said instead. "*Please*, Sawyer." It was practically a whimper at this point and Sawyer seemed about as fed up with their game as she was, so he pushed those fucking briefs off none too slowly and kicked them to the side.

There was no other word for it. He was fucking hung. Sawyer Matthews was muscled and powerful and brawny. He was a prime specimen of male in every way, from his beard to his…

Every way.

"Come here, Hollie."

She didn't wait to get asked twice. Hollie leaned up and kissed her mouth to the hot skin of his muscled thigh. Soft, dark hair tickled her cheeks and she slid her tongue over the crease of muscle that led to his groin. His cock was impossible to ignore, swollen and thick, slightly purple at the head and leaking from the tip. Unable to keep from tasting him a moment longer, Hollie leaned over and took his entire plump head into her mouth. Sawyer stumbled slightly and supported himself against the arm of the sofa, swearing as she took him deeper, deeper. He tasted of salt and fresh mountain air, cedar, the kind of hot and homey scents that made her ache to keep him close on cold winter nights.

She couldn't get him all the way down, but she could do her damnedest and she slid her tongue up and down his length, riding that delicious vein and reveling in the way lusty curse words fell unbidden from his mouth, as if he had given up holding on to any type of control.

Slowly, as if trying not to distract her, Sawyer navigated to sit on the sofa, thick legs spread, cock high in the air when she pulled back and focused on sliding her tongue over his tight balls. On an impulse, she scraped her nails across the sensitive flesh and Sawyer bucked hard at her touch.

But Hollie was all too aware that they weren't alone in the room, and she turned to face Cade, who had shucked off the rest of his clothes and was coming to kneel behind her on the rug.

"Don't mind me," he whispered, and even that capable, powerful man was starting to lose his control, starting to give over to carnal instinct. "I'm perfectly happy right back here."

With that, he slid to his knees and spread his legs apart, stroking her slick folds with ease. Hollie groaned around Sawyer's cock and he responded with a thrust that pressed him against the back of her throat. She shouldn't have liked it, but the brute masculinity was hot as hell. The very thought of being taken hard at both ends was making mini tremors pulse through her body unbidden.

"Do you want me to fuck you while you suck Sawyer's cock?" Cade asked, his voice husky with need that Hollie understood all too well. "Tell me what you want, Hollie. I'm all yours."

And in that moment, she belonged to both of them as well, free to be who she really was, here with friends from once upon a time. She pulled off of Sawyer's cock, despite his protest, and turned to face Cade.

"Fuck me," she managed. "Both of you. I want you both at the same time."

Cade barely responded, just grabbed the pants besides him and fished a condom from the back pocket. *Thank fuck one of us was thinking clearly.* From behind her came the rustle of the wrapper and a moment later his slick head was at the entrance to her throbbing pussy. Hollie tried to rock back and take him inside, but Cade's strong grip on her hips kept her still while he slid into her waiting body inch by agonizingly slow inch. He was big—not quite as big as Sawyer, but his cock was thick and hard as marble, and it filled her the way she was meant to feel, the way she had been missing for so long. When he hit a particularly sensitive spot, Hollie groaned around Sawyer's cock and he throbbed hard in response.

"Whatever the fuck you just did, do it again," Sawyer groaned. "Fuck, Hol, I'm so close."

So was she. The heat was building in her belly again and the very sensation of being filled with so much masculine power was making her body something not her own, a trigger of pleasure and need that was sure to burst again and again before the night was through.

"Are you about to come with Cade in your cunt and my cock in your throat?" Sawyer asked, the words rough and husky from his swollen lips. "You're going to come all over his cock and he's going to keep fucking you, right, princess? What are you waiting for?" He reached out and flicked one of her nipples at the same time as Cade pressed his fingers against her throbbing clit. And she did come. She came hard and fast and over and over, unable to scream around Sawyer's erection, her body writhing as the shockwaves rushed through her.

"So fucking pretty when you lose control," Sawyer said, brushing the hair from her eyes. "I want to see you to it again." At that, Cade changed his angle and Hollie's breath caught against the new onslaught of pleasure. She had *just* come. Hell, she had just come twice and still her body was on fire, aching and demanding and needing so much more than they were giving her. Sawyer's control was waning and even Cade's pace had lost some of the slow, even rhythm, instead turning into something reckless and wild, and her next release was already rising from her belly, making her breasts ache and her moans husky and wanton.

She laved Sawyer's thick erection with her tongue, sliding from root to tip before engulfing him fully, reveling in the dark groans torn from his mouth. His arms were straining with the effort to hold back and Hollie didn't want him to him. She didn't want either of them to rein it in. She wanted it all, every wide, dangerous moment of it.

But before she pulled away from Sawyer's thick erection to tell him to give over to the pleasure, to demand he accept her just as he had demanded she accept him, Hollie felt the press of Cade's thumb ringing the sensitive entrance of her ass. It made a surge of lust pound through her body and she felt as though she had just stepped out onto a very steep edge of pleasure and base, natural instinct. Ass play had always fascinated her, always called to something depraved and sinful deep inside, but the idea of being filled in all three holes at once, and by these two men, was practically enough to have her coming all over again.

Instead, she pressed back into Cade's thumb, hoping for more contact, desperate to feel him inside her tightest hole.

"Oh, sweet Hollie," he growled, as if even the stalwart good-guy cop was turning into something of a ravening beast. "You want me to finger-fuck your asshole? You want to be filled good and tight?"

She couldn't speak with her mouth full of Sawyer's erection, but her pussy tightened, and above her, Cade growled at the sensation before he sank his thumb deep into her ass.

Hollie fucking shattered. Bright lights popped hard before her eyes and she lost all sense of her body in the onslaught of overwhelming pleasure and desire and impossible need. Distantly, she heard Sawyer give a shout, then he surrendered to his orgasm, spilling hot and thick inside her mouth, which only sent her body off on a new wave of pleasure and debauchery. Behind her, Cade thrust once, twice, once more and he went still, shuddering and shaking and giving over to his own release.

Hollie came to herself slowly, and it seemed as though the men beside her did as well. Cade pulled out of her body with a gentle, careful movement and tied off the edge of the condom. Hollie watched through sleepy, half-lidded eyes as Sawyer lowered himself to the floor beside her while Cade went to dispose of the condom. Outside, the storm raged wild and hard, a harbinger of the damage that was sure to come, but it felt like nothing in comparison to the natural disaster that had just happened between the three of them.

So much for coming home and not making a big mess of things.

"Hollie." Sawyer opened his muscled, tattooed arms and she glanced up at him before deciding that they looked too inviting to turn away from. "We don't need to talk about it now. Just don't make your brain explode, okay?" It must have been the sex addling his brain, because Sawyer had been all about the 'we'll talk as soon as this is over' train of thought, but Hollie was grateful for it. She didn't have a clue where that conversation could begin and she wasn't quite ready to ruin the moment just yet.

"Maybe I should go," Cade said when he came out of the bathroom, looking slightly contrite for the powerful, controlled man he had been a moment before.

"It's storming out there, Easton," Sawyer pointed out, his gruff, mean-old way of saying that he cared, in some way shape or form, about what happened to Cade. That was a start, at least. And one Hollie could work with.

Not that she had any intention of working with anything, considering that once her work here was done, she was leaving Wolf Creek in the rearview mirror—a sobering thought, considering the incredible passion they had just shared.

"Don't leave, Cade," she said quietly, scooting over so there was room for him to lie beside her on the other side. "We can talk about all this in the morning, but just…don't leave yet, okay?"

Cade took a deep breath and glanced from Sawyer to Hollie, his dark brown gaze lingering on her, making her feel exposed and vulnerable in a way that had nothing to do with her current lack of clothing.

"We do have to talk in the morning," he said, eyeing her.

Hollie nodded. "I promise," she said. Then she shifted between the two men and closed her eyes. All of that could wait—for now, she was going to enjoy every second of the best sleep of her damn life.

Chapter Nine

Sawyer was having the best dream he'd ever had. His whole body felt good, like he'd just gone on a long run and was riding high on adrenaline and endorphins, but there was relaxed pleasure too, and his cock was hard and ready for the soft, plush ass pressing against him now. He reached for it, determined to hold it in his hands, to pull it closer and ravish the person making him feel so hot and needy. But the sensation was escaping and he distinctly began to hear a warning alarm, as if he'd tripped the wire in a museum, but this wasn't a museum and suddenly he wasn't feeling so nice and dreamy anymore and...

He sat up before he even realized he was awake, groping for a phone that wasn't on his usual bedside table or next to his bunk at the firehouse. He found it half hidden under the sofa, and he glanced down, his eyes still heavy and blurry with sleep, to see two state emergency alerts, a dozen missed text messages and two fresh calls from the station number.

Behind him, he felt movement, and when he glanced back both Hollie and Cade were fumbling for their own phones. Cade had a grim expression on his face and Hollie was muttering under her breath even while she stood and placed the phone to her ear.

"Savannah, what's the situation?"

She moved while she talked, ducking her head under the table and looking around for her clothes. The room had felt so private last night when they'd indulged their every carnal whim, but the three open windows looked out onto the expanse of the Triple Diamond Ranch and B&B.

"Hollie." She held up her hand and Sawyer tried again. "Hollie." This time, when she did look at him, he motioned to the picture window with his head. Her expression changed then immediately changed again when she ducked behind a corner not visible from the space.

"Can you repeat that, Savannah, I think my signal went out?"

Sawyer focused on finding his own pants and not the dark need he felt to hide Hollie's clothes for a good long time and keep her up in a stormy mountain lodge until they were utterly satiated. He got the impression that with a woman like Hollie he was never going to be utterly satiated, but that was well beside the point.

"What's your emergency?" Sawyer asked Cade, pulling on his pants and tying his boots in the record time it took a man of his profession.

"Camilla is down at the reservoir," Cade replied. "She says the fences are mangled pretty badly. There's an accident on 301, another one near the school, and we have several disabled vehicles downtown." Cade straightened and buttoned his shirt as he spoke. "What's your damage?"

"Trees, mostly," Sawyer replied, looking at his phone and texting his ETA back to his station at the same time. They might not have liked each other, hell, they might have been at each other's throats for years and would continue to be, this last night notwithstanding, but they had both sworn to uphold the town's safety and best interests and sometimes that meant having to act civilly enough to get the information across. "Power lines are down across town, so mitigating those will be our first task."

Hollie came out from around the corner of the room fully dressed. She pulled her hair into a tight ponytail while relaying her conversation.

"Savannah is down with Agent Flores at the reservoir," she said. "She said they're comfortable taking point on that project, but that I'm needed on the Wolf Creek bridge for washouts. Sawyer, I know we talked about you taking lead there, but focus on the downed power lines. Just lend me two of your guys and we'll be all right." She was back to being the professional hero, the woman who would run this show in the most efficient, most capable way possible, until everyone was home safe and sound. Not for the first time, Sawyer was damn glad Hollie Callihan was on his team. He pulled his phone back out of his pocket and shot off a quick message.

"Robbie and Drew will meet you down at the bridge," he said. "We'll start on Main first and work our way across town."

Hollie nodded. "Cade, I know you have accidents to triage. Both of you keep me covered and we'll reconvene here once the dust settles." She gave them both a very pointed look. "This is the first of what our predictions indicate will be a series of increasingly worse storms. Let's take it one thing at a time and use what we learn to prevent further damage as the situation increases. The more preventative measures we can take, the better off we'll be." She was right, and she was so capable that Sawyer's chest squeezed just a little in pride.

Little Hollie Callihan had never been as lost as the rest of them. She had chased adventure, followed her own path and forged a pretty damn impressive life for herself, despite the tumult and craziness. She hadn't had anyone to fall back on in her life, not really, and she'd done more than okay for herself.

So have you, Matthews.

It was something he had understood for years but was only starting to believe. Maybe it was because she was back here in this place, reminding him of so many things he'd thought he'd forgotten for good. Maybe it was simply because it was true, because out of the shadow of his home and his sadness and his desperation, something good had truly come.

The three of them started outside, fully dressed and ready to face the emergencies ahead no more than ten minutes after those initial calls. Such was the life they all led, never letting their guard down, never being vulnerable, because the second any of them did, disaster could strike.

Hollie turned to face them at the edge of the path and made eye contact first with Cade, then with Sawyer himself. Her blue eyes were brilliant and full of energy, but he knew there was more there, below the surface. There had always been more below the surface with Hollie than most of the world knew about.

"Be careful," she said, her voice quiet, but firm. "Both of you, please. Be careful."

And with that, she turned down the path toward her Jeep.

Sawyer turned to Cade Easton, the man he'd been in battle with for nearly ten years, a battle that was far from over but suddenly a million times more complicated after the night they had just shared. The look in Cade's eyes was difficult to discern, but whether they liked each other or not, Sawyer had come to know the man well since they were kids and the riot of confused emotions pulsing in his own chest was likely no different from the one in Cade's. They were going to have to talk, all three of them, when the little fires had been put out and the emergencies managed, but now was hardly the time to open that can of worms.

"Give me a call if you need any of my guys on the accidents," Sawyer said. "I'm hoping we can get these downed powerlines handled quickly then start on prep work for later this week."

Cade gave a short nod. "I'll be on the radio. Be in touch if you need us."

Then they too parted, far from friends, far even from neutral toward each other. Sawyer suspected he would never feel neutral about Cade Easton, not with all the history between them and the high emotions, but things were, undoubtedly, in a tentative truce. It would be good enough until they got their shit together. It would have to be.

He climbed into his truck and followed Cade's Bronco down to the road until they came upon the main drag and their paths diverged, Cade heading toward the interstate, where accidents awaited him, Sawyer with his own emergencies to handle.

We do rely on each other for a hell of a lot.

It was hard not to think about that when their town was facing a series of emergencies they couldn't quite anticipate the scope of. He and Cade had been at each other's throats for years, because of Hollie, because of the night neither of them had spoken of. Because of this idea they had both concocted in their own heads about whose fault it had been that she had left.

Sawyer pulled the truck up to the scene where his team was stationed, not far off the main drag from town. One of the telephone poles had been knocked sideways by a tree in the storm and canted at an angle, a handful of wires taut as they stretched between poles, a few more hanging precariously close to the ground.

"The electricity company called. We should have power off in about two minutes." Jensen had been on the team nearly as long as Sawyer himself and the man was a reliable, level-headed person a guy wanted on his side during an emergency.

"Just got the go-ahead," Lane called from behind one of the cruisers. "They're sending a team, but we can go ahead and put out the fire." It was only then that Sawyer saw the smoke from over where she was standing. He wasn't wearing his gear and from his near decade of working with his crew, he knew they could manage the fire on their own.

Still, it rankled him. The bad boy image, the tattoos and the beard and all of it, they were real to him. They kept him protected from his own demons, helped him forget the world that had left him behind because he didn't need anyone else, aside from his team, and he had long ago learned how to rely on himself. It wasn't that he never woke up in a strange bed, or even that he'd never woken in a strange bed on a night where he would have been better served to be back at the fire station. He had and he probably would again.

It was just that, while he shouldn't have stuck around the Triple Diamond Ranch, while he shouldn't have given over to whatever the fuck had happened the night before with a man he'd barely been able to tolerate for ten years and the woman who had haunted his dreams with alarming regularly, he knew that given the opportunity, he would do it all over again.

Hollie Callihan called to him. It wasn't just sexual either. Not that he didn't ache for the way she felt against him, plush and delicious and so fucking sexy. Because he did and he wanted her all over again. But he had enjoyed holding her just as much , kissing her, stroking her hair off her neck in the middle of the night. She had been the one person he had told his plans to, the one person who had seen him as more than a mistake, as more than a castoff from his deadbeat dad. When he'd been with Hollie, he'd felt like his own person, like his victories belonged to him, his emotions and his reactions were his own. He didn't need to hedge his bets or play coy. She had gotten him on day one and every day after that.

And though nearly ten fucking years had passed, though she hadn't so much as sent a postcard from her trips to Rio or Sidney or wherever the hell she had been, though the undercurrent of rage he had felt for so long at her leaving was still there, not yet satisfied, he couldn't help but admit to himself that she still had the ability to make him feel like Sawyer Matthews the man was just enough. It had taken a lot of unlearning, a lot of understanding that his father hadn't been raising him the way most fathers did, a lot of Hollie and him huddled up near the lake or wandering the Black Reef

Mountains, admitting that they felt responsible for their parents' deaths.

Only, Hollie had felt the kind of guilt of every survivor, the *why not me*, the *what if I had* and everything in between. She had been a classic case, something Sawyer had understood even when they had just been kids, their feet dangling in fresh river water — the same river water that was likely about to start barreling down on Wolf Creek. She had been innocent of everything but loving her mom and dad, and living to love them even after the robbery gone wrong. She'd been nothing but a child who cared too much.

And over months and years of friendship, she'd managed to explain the same to Sawyer. But his guilt hadn't been natural. It had been the product of grief and love. It had been created, nailed into his head by a man who had twisted his own grief into something violent.

'If you hadn't been born, your mother would still be here...' The words never truly left his mind, never quieted all that long for him to understand that they weren't true, they were the words of a madman who had nothing left in the world to care about, including his young son.

Alone, Sawyer wouldn't have been able to understand that.

But with Hollie...

She had opened his world to so very, very much and a part of Sawyer had always known that his fool heart wouldn't be so quick to let her go. So, no, it hadn't been the best for his job, for his town, for anything that had really mattered, to do what they had done last night. But there was no way he could have done anything differently.

Cade was bone weary. His body hurt and his head was starting to pound. Sleeping on the floor all night certainly hadn't helped. Neither had running accident triage for the last eight hours, but there had only been minor injuries, the cars had been taken care of and towed away and he was finally driving back to his office to drop off some papers before heading home for the day. *Finally. Finally.*

And yet, even as the prospect of a comfortable and horizontal bed — hell, the couch would do it — called his name, Cade couldn't help but admit, if only to himself, if only in the quietest part of his mind, that some of his exhaustion might not have been entirely related to the lack of sleep or the business of the day. In fact, if he looked at it just a little too close for a little too long, he could start to see threads of his emotions taking over the conversation, until he ran himself into circles. Then maybe, just maybe, right off the edge of the bridge. Or into oncoming traffic.

But *fuck*. What else was he supposed to have done? Through something silent and base and honest, he and Sawyer had taken a step the night before that had changed everything. Hell, Cade hadn't thought of Sawyer Matthews as Sawyer in years, and it already felt natural, if a little stiff, like an unusual muscle creaking back to life. But it had been *Hollie*, of all people. It had been Hollie and all at once it had been the worst and best decision he could possibly have made.

"Hey, Hoss, I was hoping to grab you before I left." Camilla met him in the hallway and they continued to walk down toward his office. Unable to keep standing much longer, Cade sank into his chair and leaned back. His shoulders relaxed ever so slightly.

"We have the reservoir report," Cam said. She handed him the sheaf of papers and settled into the chair across from his desk. Weariness etched the corners of her eyes as well and her posture wasn't the strict, rigid pose it normally was. Hell, they'd both been running straight through since the meeting last night and it was little wonder they were exhausted, though Cade had a sneaking suspicion that Camilla hadn't slept with Hollie Callihan the night before.

"Give me the elevator pitch," Cade said. "I trust you."

She smiled at that and gave a tired nod. "The water levels are higher than average for this time of year at the forebay, the mid-reservoir and the inflow. The embayment still has room, but we need to keep a close eye on it, especially if predicted rain levels prove true." She flicked through a page and continued, "No contamination in the water as of o-six-hundred today, but the Nature and Wilderness team is on high alert. We set up a sandbag perimeter off Denton Street and along the Coffee Creek side, so that should, if all goes according to plan, keep it protected during the next storm."

Cade nodded. "That's great, Cam. Thank you." He gave her a small smile. "You should go home, you look beat. I'm sure you guys didn't get too much sleep last night."

Surprisingly, Camilla's cheeks turned a rarely seen shade of bright pink and she shifted her gaze away from his. Cade blinked and tilted his head. His instinct was that he was paranoid, that everyone could see what kind of hedonism he'd gotten up to the night before, but he didn't think he was imagining the expression on Camilla's face, or those flushing cheeks.

"I meant because of the storm," he clarified, actually enjoying himself when she coughed and tried to speak.

"Right, of course. We were up late because of the storm."

"I hope you guys didn't get too wet." Oh yeah, he was starting to lose his shit if he thought that was funny, but then Camilla shot daggers at him and he couldn't help the dark laugh that escaped his mouth. She raised her eyebrow.

"You keep laughing, Sheriff," she said. "But I'm not the one walking around with a hicky on my neck."

Cade stopped laughing and pulled the camera up on his phone to check if it had been obvious to anyone who he might have come in contact with the entire day. When he didn't see anything at close inspection, however, he turned to face Camilla again, who had an expression on her face that could stop armies in their track.

"I knew it," she said. "You totally got laid last night."

"Well, so did you."

It was a rather unprofessional conversation, but he and Camilla had become more than coworkers in the last few years and he trusted her, felt to her as he would to a sister, which he had never been so lucky as to have. And, in complete honesty, it felt kind of nice that someone knew, as if it gave something real and concrete over to the whole thing, so he was no longer left wondering if it had actually happened or if he'd simply had a great fucking dream on the floor of the Triple Diamond Ranch dining room. He should have felt guilty about defiling the table, but he'd run into his fair share of Maddy Hollis and her husbands defacing furniture, and he'd definitely caught Lily, Dec and Micah with their pants down on more than one occasion, so he really couldn't bring himself to care about it all that much.

Hmm, maybe we should have the reservoir checked for pheromones…

"Don't let her break your heart again, Cade," Camilla said, her voice serious now. "You haven't let yourself care about someone in a long time and I don't want to see you give it all up for someone who doesn't appreciate it."

Cade appreciated *her*, this sprite of a woman from a powerhouse family with madness and noise and so much love. She'd adopted him right into her fold and, brusque, humorous or however her mood struck her, she kept an eye on him, listened to him, cared about him and made sure he knew it.

He'd had a family, once upon a time. Not the parents who'd birthed him. They'd been, more often than not, in a trailer home somewhere bartering for their next fix. But Cade had had a home in the wonderful Ruth Callihan and Wes and Hollie. He'd had a homecooked meals with a grandmother who wasn't his own and in care packages carefully filled with non-perishable items, as if Ruth had known that he couldn't go down to the kitchen every night, couldn't even leave his own room on the bad ones, as if she had known he was planning to make a break for it one day, that he wouldn't stick around to be hurt any longer.

Hollie had been the best part of his life. She'd come to mean a warm, soft glow, a shared bowl of popcorn, a sense of comfort and a place to hang his hat. That had made it hurt all the more when she had left, after all she knew about him, after all that she had been through at his side.

And it had made it that much harder to say no to her the night before. It hadn't even been a question. Things had just happened, just progressed until Hollie was in his arms, her face awash with pleasure.

And something deeper, something that had called to a base part of himself. Something no one, not even Camilla Flores, the woman he thought of as a sister, knew about him. But there was no doubt in Cade's mind that when Hollie had called him *Sir*, when she had done as he had asked and when she had bucked against his demands, it had been with intent and promise in her words and movements. He had seen it in her eyes that she was a woman who understood his predilections, who found her pleasure in giving up control just as he had found his in taking it. It made sense, in a way. Hollie had always been a jump-first, adventure-on-the-horizon kind of person. She had taken off for greener pastures and bigger thrills at every chance she got. His secret lifestyle might just be one she indulged in on occasion too.

That she might be a submissive both thrilled and terrified Cade. Because now that he had his head on straight, now that Camilla was voicing her concern and giving him that look that spoke volumes about all she knew about him, Cade could see how terrible an idea it had been for them to sleep together the night before. Ignoring the whole issue of another man—and that he could even manage to ignore the whole issue of another man was testament to how insane the whole thing had been—Cade knew that his relationship with Hollie had too many loose ends, too many unfinished pieces and parts and way, way too many opportunities for heartache. The last thing he needed was to want her more, or, even worse, feel this driving need for control and dominance that had him aching to make her his.

"I don't exactly want to see you get hurt either, Cam," Cade put in. Camilla had her own brothers, had people beyond him who cared for her, but he sincerely doubted she was about to tell any of them about what had undoubtedly gone down with her and Federal Emergency Agent Walsh. Savannah seemed smart and capable enough, but so had Cam's ex-girlfriend, and that hadn't ended well for anyone.

"I know, Cade," she said quietly. "And I appreciate it, but things are a whole lot less complicated between us than they are between you. I just want to make sure you're keeping yourself safe."

It was funny, that. He'd sworn an oath to protect the town, first as an incoming deputy, then as the Wolf Creek sheriff when Bob Henders had retired. Protecting people, the good folks of Wolf Creek, his friends and team, was second nature. It came to him as easily as breathing and Cade had wondered on occasion if that had played a role in why he'd taken such extreme pleasure in caring for others and bringing them to new heights, protecting them all along the way.

But he wasn't a psychologist. He was a small-town sheriff and it was a hell of a lot more important for him to focus on his job right now, and not the way that Hollie Callihan whispering the word *Sir* had made him harder than he'd ever been in his entire life.

A knock on the door dragged his surprisingly limited attention away from that particular memory, and when he called that it was open, Hollie and Savannah Walsh walked in. *Because, of course.*

It didn't escape Cade's notice that Savannah was watching Camilla intently and that Camilla, his strong, capable, take-no-prisoners friend, was blushing furiously and looking in just about every other direction. Of course, Cade only noticed that because he was doing his damnedest not to look at Hollie.

And that was the second time in a week he was glad as hell he was sitting behind his desk.

"We have some updated reports about the flood regions starting Thursday night and going into Saturday morning," Hollie said by way of greeting. "I wanted to run through them with you and Sawyer, but he's still tied up with accident cleanup, so I thought I'd leave the files with you to look at so we can meet up later. I'd also like to fax the reservoir report to my superiors, if you don't mind."

Cade nodded to the ancient fax machine in the corner of the room and Hollie pulled a file identical to the one on Cade's desk from her bag and began punching numbers into the old machine. It whirred to life and she painstakingly fed it one page at a time from the two-dozen-page report.

"What's the short take on the new reports?" Cade asked. Savannah pulled a face.

"Not better," she said. "It looks like we might get up to thirty-three percent more flooding than we were initially anticipating. We're discussing a potential evacuation, but it hasn't come to that yet. It depends more on the runoff locations for the time being." Before she could continue, her phone went off at her hip and she answered with a curt "Agent Walsh."

She took her phone call and Hollie futzed with the fax machine—which Cade was starting to believe she didn't actually have to do, that she'd just wanted an excuse to avoid making eye contact with him—and he turned to Camilla.

"You look beat. Why don't you go home and take a break until our meeting later?"

She gave him a sharp look, but it wasn't quite as sharp as usual and Cade pressed his luck. "I'm going to need you on your best game this week," he said. "That means no falling asleep on the job. Take the break now. We might not get another one any time soon."

Camilla raised her eyebrow and made to get up, collecting her things and heading for the door just as Savannah clicked off her call.

"Can you drop me at city hall?" she asked Cam when they headed toward the door. "We're discussing potential evacuation routes now." She turned to Hollie. "Lewitt says to triage with Fire and Police and I'll be in touch with what the mayor's office has to say. We may not need to evacuate yet, but she wants to know our options with this new projection."

Hollie nodded. "Do you want to take my car?" she asked. "The sheriff can drop me off when we're done here."

Cade didn't want to say no, certainly not with Camilla's eyes practically burning a hole in his head. He also didn't want to say *please don't leave me alone in this office with her* but the truth was that any time he got a second alone with Hollie, he lost his damned mind and he had a pretty good idea that things were going tits-up the second Walsh and Camilla walked out of the door.

"I don't mind dropping Agent Walsh off at the city hall, ma'am," Camilla said, her voice overly formal in what could only be compensation for the embarrassment she undoubtedly felt at whatever they had done the night before. Cade wouldn't say it out loud, but it was good for Cam to spend time with someone after all that her ex had done to her psyche, and so what if that someone happened to be one of Hollie's closest companions? "I'll make sure she gets back safely tonight too." That was softer and Hollie's gaze became a little more discerning before she nodded, bade her goodbyes and 'call me as soon as you can's and the two of them watched Cam and Savannah leave the office.

Hollie waited until they were far enough down the hall they couldn't see into the room anymore, then she closed the door behind them.

"Cade," she said, putting her hands on the desk and looking down at him. "We need to talk."

Chapter Ten

It was the kind of rush she got right before she jumped out of a plane or went on a deep-diving excursion. Her body was high on adrenaline, her heart was pumping hard, her nerves were attuned to every sensation and emotion happening around her, and yet, for all that her natural fight-or-flight instincts were kicking into high gear, Hollie was still standing in Cade Easton's office, her eyes locked with his and the privacy of the closed door making the room feel too hot and her skin feel way too tight.

"Are you sure that's a good idea, Hollie?" he asked. His gaze was difficult to read, which actually made her a little sad. Once, Hollie would have been able to tell exactly what he was thinking from a country mile. But he had changed and she had changed, and the truth was that she wasn't entirely sure she wanted to know what was on his mind at present. She already felt vulnerable, exposed and unprepared for what was to come next.

And to her own desires.

Because even just being in this room with him, Hollie's body was so alert, so ready and wanting, that it was challenging to remember why she had come in here on some pretext or another so that she might actually catch a moment with Cade alone before the proverbial shit hit the fan. With the day as busy as it had been, patching up one emergency after another and overseeing the prep work with sandbags and barriers, she hadn't been able to spend too much time thinking about all that had transpired the night before. But when she and Savannah had reconvened at her once favorite hotspot, Debbie's Diner, an old-school eatery with the best burgers in town, her defenses had been down, her adrenaline had left her and she had started thinking about everything that had come to pass.

And regretting it.

Well, not so much regretting it as…

She wasn't entirely sure. She knew without question that they should not have slept together, certainly not all three of them in a public location at the Triple Diamond Ranch of all places, though according to small-town rumor, the new owner was hardly the discreet type, and she had some good old-fashioned ribbing to do next time she saw Dec and Micah.

Entirely beside the point.

The point being…the point being that Cade looked really fucking hot with the top button of his uniform undone, his shirtsleeves rolled up and that expression on his face that said he knew exactly what she was thinking. And so, exactly *without* thinking, Hollie blurted out the first thing that came to her mind.

"Are you a Dom?"

She stuffed her hands over her mouth as if she was in a cartoon and could just take the damn stupid question back. But Cade blinked slowly, his eyes so discerning now, his full lips parting just a little, and Hollie knew there was no coming back from the question.

"That's what you wanted to talk about?" he asked.

She shook her head. "Not even a little bit. I came to say that last night was a mistake."

He raised an eyebrow and leaned back in his chair. "Was it?"

She hadn't been expecting that and it frazzled her. "I mean, not exactly. I don't have any regrets, but I know we shouldn't have made that choice. I know it wasn't a good idea."

"Why?" His voice was so measured and calm that she didn't exactly need an answer to her previous stupid-ass question.

"I'm leaving, Cade," she said, standing up from the desk and pacing around the room for want of something to do with her manic energy.

I can think of someone *to do. Or someones.*

"I'm leaving as soon as this job is over and I'm never coming back here. Gram's gone, Wes is off gallivanting around the world."

"You still pay for the house," he pointed out. She turned to face him.

"How do you know that?"

Cade gave her a knowing look. "You do know that I'm the sheriff, right?" he asked, as if she hadn't been watching the shiny star on his badge to avoid those devastating deep brown eyes.

"It hadn't escaped my notice," she said drily.

"So why, Hol?" he asked, ignoring her sarcastic tone. "Why pay for the house you'll never come back to? There must be a reason."

A reason that had her wishing they were back at the question about whether or not he was a Dom.

"Drop it, Cade," she said fiercely.

"Fine." He stood and leaned against the desk and God how could she not be reminded of all they had done last night, half of which in a very similar position to this one? "I'll drop that, but I will say this — you have more reasons to return here than just your gram and Wes."

"It's not home anymore." And if her voice wobbled a little bit when she said it then Hollie wasn't going to start asking herself why.

"You keep telling yourself that," he said, and God, when had he gotten so close to her, that masculine power overwhelming and confident even as he stood before her, nothing outwardly different in his demeanor but the tension in the room somehow so much higher? Hell, she'd always been so turned to him that it had only been a matter of time between them. "And maybe you'll start to believe it."

I'm not supposed to want him, and definitely not supposed to want him again.

But hell and damnation, she did. Last night's indulgence hadn't been the itch-scratching she'd hoped for. It had been a taste of what she had been craving for so, so long and her body ached for more of the debilitating pleasure by simply being around him.

And yet, there was also that gut-deep part of her that felt almost *guilty*, as if she were being unfaithful to Sawyer, in a way, which was completely crazy considering there was nothing going on between the two of them, or the three of them, and certainly nothing that warranted her faithfulness and certainly nothing that should be worthy of a guilt trip.

"The Cabaret and Collar."

Hollie narrowed her eyes. It wasn't the oddest thing to have happened in the last two days, but she hadn't exactly expected prim and proper Cade Easton to be saying words like that, and in that particular tone of voice. Then again, she hadn't expected him to be demanding and determined the night before as he fucked her from behind while she took Sawyer's cock in her mouth…

"The Cabaret and Collar?" she repeated. Her mind was already foggy with the images of how she must have looked all spread out and wanton, and it was difficult to find the thread back to the conversation.

"The first club I ever went to," he explained. "And where I learned I was a Dom." He was staring at her intently now, as if prodding her to say something about his needs. "You asked and it's about time we started being honest with each other, so yes. I am a Dom. For the right partners and within the right context."

Hollie knew there was some kind of proper response, something informed and respectful and maybe even insightful. She knew that as the rational, capable woman she was. But the rational side of her, the part of her mind that was so accustomed to making smart, logical decisions, had abdicated in favor of the base 'jump first and ask questions later' side that had first had her fleeing this small town and sent her jumping, climbing and diving since.

"And unless I'm much mistaken…" Cade continued, coming to stand before her so that he pinned her against the desk with a strong hand on either side of her waist. It was all Hollie could do not to buck her hips into his. "You quite enjoy being told what to do." His mouth was at her ear now and so close she could nearly feel the way his plush lips shaped each of the words. This was madness, giving in to this desire of theirs, but Hollie couldn't see it as a choice. It was the only thing she could do. Walking away from everything Cade Easton had to offer simply wasn't an option.

"What about Sawyer?" she asked, because the one still functioning part of her brain, the part that wasn't preoccupied with her tightening nipples and her throbbing pussy, that part of her was still able to remember all the complicated things that made this affair so incredibly dangerous — and incredibly enticing.

"He isn't here right now," Cade said quietly. The words were a statement of fact, but that didn't absolve Hollie of the roiling guilt conflicting with the heated desire pulsing through her body.

"Cade, I need to know how this all works." There, she still had it in her to be capable of giving a directive.

"I don't honestly know, Hollie," he said, and in that moment Hollie knew she would do just about anything to take the sadness and doubt out of this man's heart and voice. "But I do know that I want you, like I've never wanted anything, that you're the woman who believed in me, who taught me what it meant to have a family, the woman who helped me take a leap when I would have stayed on the shore. So yes, I want you — all to myself. But if you need to go speak with Sawyer after I have you against my desk, then I'll say I understand and leave it at that."

Her mind was whirling and overwhelmed with all that he had said in such a short turn of phrase. Cade had been as much part of her home growing up as Wes or Gram had been, as the tire swing in the backyard, as tuna casserole on Thursday nights. He might not have even realized it, but he had taught her just as much about a place to plant roots as she had supposedly taught him.

Hollie brought her hand up to his cheek and her heart nearly burst when he pressed the stubbled skin back into her touch. Coming back to Wolf Creek hadn't just been dangerous. It had been a no-turning-back leap into the past and a questionable future all at once, and Hollie had no idea what that meant.

"You've always been my family," she said, almost so quietly that she couldn't hear it herself. So few people in her new life knew of her past and she had kept it that way, locking secret desires and needs up in a box in the attic of her mind, never to be opened. But telling Cade all that he had meant to her then, all he had come to mean to her in just a few days together, felt as natural to Hollie as swimming deeper or climbing higher. "Cade, you completed our dining room table. I'll never forget that."

"But," he probed and his eyes were a dark brown, loaded and hot and making it very challenging for her to continue along her train of thought.

"But I'm confused," she admitted. "What we shared last night was a lot. And I don't regret it, truly, but decisions have repercussions."

"Maybe," Cade admitted, his voice taking on that gravelly, demanding tone that sent sparks of heat straight to her pussy and made Hollie involuntarily arch to be closer to him. "But for right now, can't we just enjoy the spoils?"

You're already in the water. Might as well enjoy yourself before the storm.

Hollie didn't think, not anymore, not about the complicated web of emotions and desires she was weaving herself into, not about the way she had felt so protected and cared for while sleeping between the two men on the least comfortable floor in the state, not about the extremely intimate expression that Savannah and Camilla Flores had shared on their way out of Cade's office. She only took her opportunity and did what she so desperately ached to do. She kissed Sheriff Cade Easton.

He allowed her the lead for a moment, then he took over, leaning in to her body so that Hollie was pressed against the desk and grinding into him, so that she could wrap her legs around his waist and pull him as close to her needy, throbbing center as possible. She ached for him, for more of his touch, for more of the sweet, desperate pleasure to give way to release, but Cade drove a hard bargain and Hollie knew that he wouldn't let her get what she wanted so easily, not a snowball's chance in hell.

"One day, I'm going to take you on a real bed," Cade whispered in her ear. "The way you deserve to be loved, Hollie."

One day, as if they had all the time in the world, as if the threat of literal natural disasters wasn't looming on the horizon, as if she wasn't an emergency preparation professional walking into unmitigated destruction and chaos with full awareness and no evacuation plan. For now, it was just her and Cade, the way he felt trailing kisses along the slope of her neck, then pulling down the zipper on her windbreaker, then brushing his mouth over her collarbone.

He bit the skin there and she groaned, reveling in the mingling pain and pleasure of the movement and the way her body ached for so much more than one bite.

"You're going to get it," Cade whispered, "I promise." And Hollie realized she had been demanding more out loud. She gasped when his fingers skated her tank top and found her swollen nipples through the fabric. When he squeezed almost too hard, her whole body wracked with unmitigated pleasure and her need for more, for so much more, hiked, sped up and slowed down all at once, as if Cade was playing some sort of ballad against her body that only he knew the music for and she was simply along for the ride.

His fingers found the button of her jeans and he slowly began drawing them open. The slightest pressure around where she desperately wanted him was a teasing touch, not nearly enough to help her find the release she craved, intentionally pushing her higher and closer to that edge without ever getting near to falling. He pulled the zipper free one tooth at a time, then hooked his hands into the loops of her belt and slowly helped her to wiggle out of her jeans. Hollie kicked her boots off and Cade bent to push the pants off her legs, tossing them and her emergency standard wool socks off and to the floor somewhere that didn't matter.

"Do you trust me, darlin'?" he asked, starting to trail kisses up her bare leg, that sinful, promising drawl betraying his own arousal.

Hollie nodded, so very aware of her own lust, her lips and skin swollen and flush, her face undoubtedly a map of need and willingness, her legs spread, exposing soaked panties to the man who could do whatever he pleased to her desperate body.

"I do," she managed, past the haze of need, an instinct kicking in before she even realized what it was. "*Sir*."

Cade's eyes went even darker. The proper police officer veil dropped away and he took up the mantle of his dominant personality. It felt so right, in this moment, to be at his mercy and to have him at her own as they explored their baser desires in a give-and-take game of trust and need.

"Oh, you sweet thing," he murmured. "I'm going to reward you for being so good." He stepped back away from her body and Hollie groaned in displeasure at the lack of pressure. Cade simply raised one eyebrow and she hushed, taking his lead and following it without question.

"Turn around, darlin'," he murmured, his voice clear and controlled. "And take off your jacket."

She shed the jacket as quickly as she could, then turned to present herself to him, her arms against the desk, her legs spread wide and her head bent in the natural pose she felt so at home in.

"Fuck, you're beautiful," Cade muttered, and she loved that note of desperation he allowed to slip through. "I'm going to fill you up, Hollie, you know that, right?"

She nodded, the words playing havoc with her sanity and making her want more than just touches and glances.

"Please, Sir," she managed, "Touch me. Oh fuck, please touch me."

"I don't think so," Cade replied, and she heard him settle into the seat across from where she stood. "I'd much rather see you work for it." He paused and the silence was weighty and thick with tension. "The reward is so much greater when you've earned it, don't you agree?" She most definitely did *not* agree right at that moment, when her arousal was seeping through her panties and making the insides of her quivering legs slick with need. But she also knew that the relief she desperately sought would be that much harder won if she went against Cade's requests, so she nodded and kept her head bowed.

"Yes, Sir," she managed, though there was no denying the need in her voice. Cade didn't seem to have any problem with it.

"I'm going to tell you exactly what I'm going to do to your sweet, wet body," he explained, detached and controlled in a way that had Hollie desperate to break down every single one of his defenses. "And if you don't come by the time I'm finished, you'll be rewarded. Do you understand?"

Oh, she understood. She understood that Cade had figured out her number in just five minutes and had picked a game he was certain to win.

"Sir." Pleading had never helped, but, God, even the promise of such delicious torture had her rubbing her legs together in desperation.

"Spread your legs wide," he told her. "And keep them apart. I want to see how wet your panties are when you beg me for a single touch, a single finger in your hot, slick cunt, when I tell you how I'm going to take you from behind in one thrust because your body is so willing and open to me."

Hollie moaned—she couldn't help the sound that escaped and she could practically feel the smile Cade gave in return.

"That's right, Hollie. You'll be moaning for my cock, begging me to drive your body harder and deeper, to fill your mouth with my fingers or to spread your cheeks wide and slide my thick, heavy cock across your tight hole. Tell me, sweet one, is that what you want?"

Hollie nodded, barely trusting herself to speak for fear of that begging and because she knew he would be able to tell from the first word how close to the edge she was, how incredibly close she was. If she just rocked forward a little bit…

"Are you rubbing yourself against my desk?" Cade asked, and the son of a bitch almost had a note of humor in his voice. "Are you so desperate to come that you're rubbing your swollen cunt against my desk? Tell me, Hollie, tell me how badly you need my cock in your tight cunt?"

Her response was guttural and she clenched the desk so hard her fingers ached, but there was nothing she could do, nothing she could say except to give over to the harsh and penetrating pleasure that rioted through her body and left her gasping for air. Wave after wave of need crashed over her, and bright light burst when she shut her eyes hard against her own release. Finally, finally, the lust began to roll back and she pushed up slightly from the desk, aware that Cade was standing beside her now, lifting her chin with one strong finger and looking at her as if she were a feast after forty years in the desert.

"You sweet girl," he murmured, "I'm going to take great pleasure in punishing you." He walked to the other side of his desk and fished around in one of the drawers until he found what he was looking for—a thick, wooden ruler that he held with the confidence of a man accustomed to the weight and power in his hands.

"I know how much you love to walk the line of pleasure and pain, control and surrender," he said, coming back to stand at her side, "so let's walk it together. If you can take my punishment without surrender, hold on tight to yourself and to my demands, then I'll fuck you right here against this desk. How do that sound?"

Like fucking heaven. Even though she had just come, Hollie's body was vibrating with the need this man inspired within her and her pussy clenched on emptiness as he continued to promise her all that she most wanted.

"Very fair, Sir," she replied. "Thank you."

"Oh, it will be my pleasure," Cade replied. He came to stand behind her and continued. "Count and thank me for your punishment," he said. "And remember yourself. Don't give in or you'll have to leave." No part of Hollie wanted to walk outside his office without feeling him again, in and around her body, so she nodded and prepared for the first slap.

It came without warning, simple and controlled, as if Cade had put the setting to two on the scale and was warming her up. Still, the sting of the wooden ruler against her lace-clad ass had Hollie bucking hard against the desk and trying to ride the wave of pain and pleasure before it abated.

"One, thank you, Sir." At that, he delivered his next spank, then his next, each getting just a little bit harder, each followed by the number and her thanks for all that he was giving her, for all that he asked of her.

"I don't believe this is quite enough punishment," Cade said, his voice almost introspective, once they had reached five. He placed the ruler beside her hand on the desk and with an agonizing slowness began sliding her panties down her legs until Hollie was able to step out of them and kick them to the side. He trailed his hand up her leg and she tried to get more of that desperately needed contact, and Cade let her, cupping her sopping pussy with one strong hand that just wasn't enough, fuck, fuck, *fuck*, wasn't anywhere near enough.

Then, when he pressed two fingers deep inside her cunt, Hollie nearly screamed from the pleasure, but she held on, desperate for the bigger prize, for the way he felt inside her, for so much more than just fingers.

"Hold still, sweet girl," he said, before picking up the ruler once more and, fingers still deep inside her, swatted her bare, exposed ass. Hard. Hollie ground her teeth to keep from giving over to the pleasure, but Cade noticed when she clenched around his fingers.

"You're so fucking tight," he said, sliding in and out of her and brushing her clit with feather-light touches when he did. "I can't wait to slide inside you, Hollie. I can't wait to have you."

She was losing her mind and his promises were growing richer and more demanding.

"Then have me," she wasn't quite begging, but she was close.

"Not quite yet," Cade replied. He slid her fingers free of her pussy and pulled back to slowly, almost gently, spread her ass cheeks apart. Hollie sucked in a tight breath. She had long discovered that pushing that particular boundary was an effective way to have her coming in five seconds flat and she had the sneaking suspicion that Cade knew that all too well.

He pressed one of his slick fingers against her hole and she yielded to him with ease, allowing him past the ring of muscle to fill her with one, then two fingers, sliding in and out of her tightest hole with movements that made bright lights flash before Hollie's eyes.

Then he brought the ruler down on her ass. Hollie clenched her teeth so hard she could feel the blood pumping through her entire body, in time with the rhythm of her mind chanting *more, more, more,* but she wouldn't surrender, not this time, not with what Cade had demanded of her, not with all she had to prove to him, to give to him.

"Good girl," he managed, though his voice too was thick with desire and Hollie ached to make him lose control, ached to have him give over to his baser instincts, to take her body hard and to surrender as much to her as she did to him. "Three more."

One slap and her body reverberated with the pain and pleasure of it, sparks of lust rioting up her spine and making her shake in his arms.

Two slaps and she almost collapsed then and there, the precipice of release right under her foot and crumbling more quickly than she could move back.

Three slaps and Hollie's pussy convulsed. Her nipples tightened to painful points. A needy, carnal groan tore from her throat and still she clenched the desk and held on for dear life against the onslaught of pleasure. With a rough, shaky voice, she thanked Cade and rested her head against the desk.

He withdrew with care, each digit a powerful trigger for her need and lust and she held her breath until she was empty again.

"You deserve that reward, sweet one," he murmured, and she heard the sounds of him tearing open a condom wrapper and unzipping his pants. A moment later, he was pressed against her entrance, hard and throbbing and everything Hollie had ever wanted. She pushed back against him and it spoke volumes to how on edge Cade was because he let her, meeting her body's movements halfway until he was seated inside her, his cock thick and hard and filling her in all the right ways.

"Cade," she managed, her voice husky and rough as it drew out his name, sparking with pleasure and need.

He placed a hand upon hers on the desk and threaded their fingers together when he pulled out of her body.

"I know, Hol," he murmured, no longer in control, no longer in command, just Cade and Hollie and the beauty of what their bodies did when they came together. "I know, you beautiful girl."

She felt beautiful and like herself again in each pull of his body and push of her own flesh against Cade's. The complications, the challenges and the history between them could be forgotten, just for the moment, as he gave and took and she gave and took and they met each other in a mutual, building pleasure that took Hollie right to the edge.

"Let go, darlin'," Cade said. "You can let go. I'm right behind you." He reached around her waist and slid his fingers against the heat of her throbbing clit, swiping slow and steady until Hollie couldn't hold on for a second later and she did let go, her release a slow-motion collapse of control, an implosion that started in her toes and climbed higher and higher until her body was trembling, then shaking, then she was falling right over the edge into a deafening, beautiful, unseen pleasure, the likes of which she had only known once in her life.

Cade followed right behind her, and she distantly felt him pump once, twice against her slick walls before his breathing began to slow and he rested his chin against her shoulder, coaxing her back to the room and the world around them.

"Are you okay?" Cade asked, sliding off her body. He pulled the condom free and tossed it before he buttoned up his pants. Then he found her lace panties and jeans beside his desk and tugged the legs right side out before handing them to her. Hollie slowly dressed, her limbs still boneless with the after-effects of her pleasure, and Cade picked her jacket up off the ground and hung it from the back of the chair in front of her.

"I'm more than okay," Hollie said honestly. She was, in a way. But the connection between them was so real, so raw that it frightened her too, made her wonder if taking that first step hadn't been her undoing, if there was any way return to how things had been without imagining and wishing for something else for her entire life. "Are you okay?"

Cade smiled, that aw-shucks, boy-next-door smile he'd given her so many times in her life. The smile that had once been like walking through the kitchen door of her gram's home on a sticky summer night, like the grassy blanket of backyard between her toes, like stringing dollar store lights around a plastic Christmas tree with the old radio on.

Cade didn't need any prompting. He walked up to her, gathered her in his arms and simply held her, simply gave her the structure she needed to keep standing in that moment.

"I'm scared too, Hol. I'm scared too."

Amazingly enough, they were exactly the words she needed to hear.

Chapter Eleven

"I'm not saying everyone should do it. I'm just saying it could be more common if people accepted that sex and mutual love between more than two people is normal."

Hollie backed into the Triple Diamond Bed and Breakfast dining hall butt first, carrying a tray of coffees and a stack of sheets Lewitt and the team in Denver had sent to them.

"Who's having mutual love?" she asked, hoping her voice sounded normal and not like she'd been the recipient of mutual love right on the floor and — *mmm*, that table right there — only two nights before.

Lily took the stack of papers balanced in the crook of Hollie's arm and continued the rant Hollie had walked in on.

"It's normal here," she said. "I mean, no one in this town has looked twice at either of us for having nontraditional relationships, but D.C., the big bad city...."

Given that Lily was from San Francisco, another big, hotshot coastal city, Hollie was inclined to think that the city was not the actual enemy of the people.

Maddy, Lily's older sister and the calmer of the Hollis sisters, accepted a cup of coffee and donut from the tray Hollie had set down on the table and she leaned back against the table — fuck, *that* table — and explained.

"Our friend Ev is starting to go public with her relationship and some people are struggling with it," she said. "Lily's got it in her head that everyone in the world wants some sort of polyamorous relationship, and while I don't believe that's true, I do think we're a largely conventional society and it's incredibly detrimental to our progress." She took a bite and powdered sugar dusted her lips, giving her a youthful, girlish appearance. Maddy and Lily both had a few years on her, but suddenly Hollie felt old and world-weary.

"Why do you think Wolf Creek is so okay with it?" she asked. "When I was growing up here, people took issue if a kid was poor, didn't hardly look past that."

Not *everyone* had taken issue with a kid being poor. And she'd had her friends, even, outside of Sawyer and Cade. But still, she had known how they looked at the kids bussed over from the other side of town. Even when they had first moved to Wolf Creek and she'd barely been old enough to go to grammar school, she'd noticed.

Lily and Maddy both seemed to contemplate that for a long moment and it was Lily who replied.

"People here are a salt-of-the-earth type," she said finally. "The sky is bigger, you know. There's less noise and things here, they're real, good things. Soil, sky, rain, life and death." She smiled. "Love."

It was no question that Lily Hollis was in love. And Hollie knew both Micah and Dec fairly well, for all her track record of leaving friends behind when she went. Neither of them was the kind of man to roll over and take something they weren't okay with. They were both powerful and capable in their own rights and if they were in some sort of unconventional relationship with Lily, it was because they both wanted to be.

"Lily just wants everyone to run around with two boyfriends and keep the balance of the universe," Maddy teased. Lily chucked a powered donut at her and it hit Maddy square in the chest, an explosion of sugar bursting across her dark red sweater.

"I'll get you for that," Maddy said, but Lily had grabbed the box of donuts and was stepping out of reach.

"For the record, no you won't." That was directed at Maddy. "And I don't want everyone to have two boyfriends. I said two partners. Let's be inclusive here, Mads."

The women devolved into childish squabbling and it made Hollie think of her own wayward sibling, off somewhere saving the world, out of contact, and suddenly Hollie missed him in a way she hadn't in some time.

"I think it's hard for some people to understand," she said after a moment, breaking up the fight before it could become a serious wrestling match. The Hollis women were slight but that didn't mean a whole hell of a lot of anything when it came to fighting sisters.

"From the outside, yes," Lily said, settling into the chair beside them with her cup of coffee and seemingly undisturbed by the chunk of hair that had come free from her fishtail braid in the tussle. "And yes, it's unconventional. Listen, when Maddy told me about Ryder and Christian, I wasn't sure what to make of it. And Maddy and I have been through a hell of a lot." She paused to give her sister a meaningful glance, and just like that their fight was over and they were back to being best friends. And if Hollie felt a pang of envy at that, it was neither here nor there.

"But as I was falling love with Dec and Micah, Hollie, there was no other option. In fact, they tried to get me to choose between the two of them at one point and I was so angry I rode off into the woods and nearly got my sorry ass killed." A dark expression crossed her face, but Lily just shook her head and continued. "It's just love. What's so wrong about that?"

Nothing. Nothing's wrong about love.

Except that Hollie had struggled to understand what love looked like after moving away. She'd never been in a serious relationship. Wes was the only family that she had left and he was gone more of the time than he was home. She loved her parents and she had loved her gram, desperately. But the kind of soul-bearing, full-sacrifice love that Lily spoke of for Dec and Micah was foreign to her and it made that ache in her heart a little more intense and sad.

Maybe it's not so foreign as all that.

She tried to hush the voice in her head, but it wasn't as easy to tune out as the Hollis sisters bickering and Hollie couldn't ignore the idea that she had felt a deep affection — perhaps a love of sorts — for both Cade and Sawyer when they had just been kids. It was hard not to wonder then, if she gave it more time, if she allowed this thing between them, to, fuck, she didn't even know, to unfold, then what would things look like? How would she move forward in her life knowing she cared for them, had always cared for them and they hadn't stopped caring for her?

"How does it work?" she asked before she could stop herself. The curious expressions on both Lily's and Maddy's faces were telling of how enthusiastic her tone had been.

"Why, exactly?" Maddy asked, and goodness, that was an older sister voice if Hollie had ever heard one. She had one older brother and had never been an older sister herself, but the tone was unmistakable.

"I'm just curious about the logistics," she said, shrugging her shoulder as if to say, 'I work in logistics and emergency preparation and navigating multiple partners are the same thing.'

Which they were turning out to be.

"The logistics are different for everyone," Maddy explained patiently. "For me, Christian and Ryder were already up for nontraditional relationships. Lily had to work every step of the way to get her guys to see what was right in front of their faces. Our friend Ev, she was in a partnership and they invited a third in—these things happen from any angle."

And what if they hate each other?

It was a question she didn't dare ask, given how many people knew full well of the temper tantrums between the two men who had been occupying her thoughts and dreams for two days. Not that she was willing to admit it—but there really was no use in lying to herself.

But before she could press further, the far door to the dining hall pushed open and Christian and Ryder came in, carrying large kegs and boxes filled with bottles, to fill the bar at the far wall of the dining hall.

"Micah has your truck for the day," Christian said to Lily. They placed the heavy cargo down on the ground like it weighed nothing at all.

Imagine how much more convenient it would be to have two of those men cleaning my place.

Hell and damnation, one was good. She wanted one. No, she didn't even want one. The sparse Denver apartment, still half-unpacked after nearly three years, was not the kind of place where one took a man after a date.

"I'm sure he did," Lily said under her breath and she faux-whispered to Hollie, "My truck is brand new and much nicer so I'm saddled with an old Ford lemon and he's going to go enjoy 375 horsepower."

Before Hollie could reply, Ryder continued, "Also, we got a radio signal that the fire chief is ready for an evacuation test if you want to go down to the fire station or have him come up here."

Ryder probably knew exactly what he was saying when he said *come up here*, but Hollie elected to ignore it in favor of the more pressing responses.

"I'll head on down to the station," she said, the room in which they had gotten naked and made love for hours before an open fire suddenly feeling rough and challenging to navigate.

She gathered up her belongings and tried not to think too much about the conversation she had shared with the Hollis sisters as she navigated her Jeep down the hill toward the Wolf Creek Fire Station across town. Remnants from the night of the first storm were still visible in the felled trees and large puddles of water at the edge of the road, and it made the guilt roil in her stomach alongside the confusion and frustration. She was here to do a job—a job she loved and was damn good at—and all she could think about was the way that Lily and Maddy made it seem so damn easy to fall in love with more than one man at a time.

Not that she was in love. Because she wasn't.

She had been—once upon a time she had felt the love of youth and innocence, the love of friendship and companionship. That love had bloomed and burst into something more, something terrifying and real, something that had sent her running far, far away without leaving a trace. And now it was time to atone for her cowardly actions.

Hollie was so caught up in her own dangerous thoughts that she barely noticed the drive across town until she pulled up in front of the fire station. One of the engines was in the bay and the other open door was empty, leading her to believe that one of the teams was out doing cleanup before the worst of the storms came to hit. She parked, took a deep breath and headed inside the station, unsure of what she would find when she met with Sawyer alone. Her last meeting with Cade hadn't exactly gone the way she had intended, and while her mind was awash of confusion and nerves, her body was responding to the idea of seeing Sawyer again with something akin to desperation.

It's been a while. It's nothing.

But Hollie couldn't lie to herself. It had been a while before coming to town, but certainly not long enough to turn her body molten at the very idea of a secret moment with Sawyer. He had done something to her, something completely different and entirely as delectable as Cade's something, and it made her crave for base desires she had no right to indulge.

"Chief, you here?" she called into the garage, hoping she wouldn't have to find him up in his office, where the door shut and the likelihood of her keeping control over her own desperate whims decreased by the second.

"Come on up," he called, his rough, deep voice echoing around the empty room. She climbed the stairs and stopped short at the sight of Fire Captain Sawyer Matthews wearing only a pair of blue jeans.

He was turned away from her, and his back was a map of thick, capable muscles and spiraling ink, beautiful, haunting designs, forms she wanted to trace with her tongue and her fingers and her lips.

On the top of one shoulder was the town's symbol, a silhouette of a wolf at the bottom of the Black Reef Mountain Range, the same mountains threatening to flood them where they stood. A single word curled over the wolf's back.

Home.

Her heart began to thud in her chest so loudly Hollie briefly wondered if Sawyer could hear it. Despite all that he had survived, all he had lived through with his son-of-a-bitch dad, Sawyer had still made Wolf Creek the place he went for that sense of returning. He had still turned the land and open sky into his home, even with the memories.

And though she had grown up with love and connection and support, though things had been good for her — if hard, still good — Hollie hadn't been able to make such a home of this town.

Or so she had always believed.

Before she could tear her gaze from the image to the other designs adorning his back, Sawyer turned around. It took all Hollie's control not to let her jaw drop open at the sight of him. Sure, they had been more than intimate just a few days before, but things had all happened so quickly and they hadn't removed much clothing before succumbing entirely to the heat and lust burning them all up. But now, in the bright light of the firehouse bunker, with just the two of them and too much time stretching in the space between, Hollie couldn't stop looking. His arms and shoulders were thick with power and his chest rippled with the kind of strength born from use, from hauling trees and carrying heavy fire hoses and saving lives.

The front of his chest had even more ink than his back, and Hollie focused on those designs rather than the smirk totally stretching across Sawyer's face right now.

"You have a lot more tattoos than I remember," she said, trying to sound light and most definitely not admitting to him with just the tone of her voice how much she wanted to lick each and every one of those tattoos.

"A lot has changed since you last saw me," he said, and images came unbidden to Hollie's mind of summers spent running through the woods and swinging into the lakes at the base of the mountain. Wolf Creek hadn't bothered with a town pool, but on the hot, hot days of summer they had crowded those lakes and she had spent her formative years in the sunshine and blue-green water, dodging fish and Wes' splashing. In her memories, Sawyer was just as tall, but he was lankier then, still a boy growing into his manhood, even with early lines of ink on his skin, ones he had gotten the day he had turned eighteen, ones she had stood by him as he'd winced through.

There was no denying that he was all man now, and that the thick curl of dark red hair that nearly brushed his shoulders and the beard she had tugged on just two nights before, were delicious, masculine and begging for her touch all over again.

"I got one to remember you," he said, his voice soft and almost gentle. Sawyer had so much gentleness in him, freckles across almost rosy cheeks that belied the sweetness of such a large, powerful man.

Hollie couldn't speak, not to reply and not when Sawyer took the two steps closer to her and slowly pushed the side of his jeans down just enough to show a small holly sprig. It was done in the style of a classic botanical book, and the dark ink and shading contrasted with Sawyer's light skin in a beautiful, almost artistic way.

Hollie couldn't help herself. She reached out and stroked the ink, the skin right above where his flank shifted and led to more intimate terrain — a path she so desperately wanted to follow.

"Why?" she asked instead, looking up to his eyes and realizing he was so much closer to her than he had been just a moment before. "I left — I…" She looked away, no longer able to keep his gaze. "I don't deserve it."

Sawyer took a deep breath.

"It was my graduation present for you," he said quietly. "I was going to show you that night, but…" He trailed off and Hollie was grateful for it. They both knew full well that had been the night she'd packed a bag and driven out of town, and she wasn't entirely certain she could hear those words on his lips and not feel them directly to her heart.

"I think we need to talk," she said, because this was torture, this standing before one of the men she had cared about most in the world and not being able to say a damn thing, not being able to explain how much he meant to her but that they still couldn't be together, not for real, not in the way she could only dream about.

"Damn right we need to talk," he said. "But first…" He walked through a door beside the bunkroom and came out with a manila folder straining at the seams. "We ran these two evacuation plans like you asked. I'm holding off the third until my team comes back from a call in Wilborn."

Hollie took the plans and put them into the bag at her hip, acknowledging that she was dawdling.

"Any unforeseen complications?" she asked. She'd run a thousand evacuations in her time and there were always unforeseen complications, but if they did their job right, then no one would be the wiser for it.

"We ran into some snags on the bridge road when we tested the second route," Sawyer replied. "We'd have to give more stagger time or it's going to back up, and we don't want passengers on the bridge when the river rises."

She made a quick note of it in her phone, then turned to him. "Okay then," she said. "Should we do this thing?"

Hollie made it sound like they were going into battle, and Sawyer had to resist the urge to laugh. Hollie Callihan was a woman who didn't fear much. She was an adventurous spirit and he had always admired that about her — admired it until she had used that same spirit to head for distant shores. But that the idea of discussing emotions, of talking about the way she felt, was so terrifying to her was almost funny. It would have been, if it didn't scare Sawyer just as much.

He hadn't been raised with feelings. He had been raised only with the idea of fear and control and never giving in. Learning how to come out of that sense of proving himself, of fighting everything and going hard with anger and a devil-may-fuck-off attitude, that had been hard won. He would hardly call himself a paragon of emotional stability, but he had a far better relationship with his emotions now than he had ever had before.

"I'm not going to bite," he said, suddenly needing to lighten the mood, though he wasn't entirely certain why. He still harbored that anger toward her — even as it lessened by the day with the knowledge that Hollie really didn't understand all she had left behind. Running due to fear was absolutely something Sawyer could appreciate it. "Unless you ask nicely."

She tried to give him a stern look, but it was undermined by the flash of heat he saw in her eyes, and Sawyer's cock pulsed behind his jeans. God, she was pretty. Even with her hair pulled into a ponytail and that ridiculous regulation FEMA windbreaker, Hollie made his mouth go dry and his baser instincts take the wheel.

"Sawyer."

"What do you want me to say, huh?" he asked. "Hollie, you were the person I always thought would be at my side. You were the person who made me believe I was more than my dad's by-blow, okay, more than the shit hand dealt to me. I didn't know what the fuck to think when you suddenly turned back up in this podunk town and I don't know how to stop myself from wanting you." He has almost let slip those damn dirty words, the words he hadn't said the night she had left, the words he only thought about in the dark of night when he wondered where he had gone wrong.

I don't know how to stop myself from loving you.

But if there was ever a way to scare off a woman for whom a cave dive was more enticing than commitment, it was saying those ridiculous little words.

"You love this town," she said quietly. "And you've always been more than what your father made you believe. He was a right bastard, Sawyer, everyone knew it."

"And I do too," he said. "Because of you, Hol." He ran his hand through his hair and couldn't help but notice that her eyes followed his movements. He hoped she was thinking of their night in the dining hall, because he hadn't stopped thinking about it in days and it was starting to seriously mess with his life. But Hollie Callihan messing with his life wasn't exactly breaking news.

"I didn't do anything," she said quietly.

"Exactly," Sawyer replied. "You treated me like a normal kid, like some punk-ass teen with something to prove. You let me be who I was outside of my situation, Hollie. No one else did that."

She hadn't asked about his dad, not once in their entire friendship. It had been entirely understood that he had an ear to listen and a place to lie if he ever needed it, but she hadn't pushed or looked at him differently or done anything other than be his friend when the rest of the world had been examining him through a microscope and passing judgment.

"You helped me just as much," she said quietly. "Wasn't exactly like the transition was easy." How could it have been, moving from the big city to a small ranching town after losing both her parents? What could possibly have been easy about that? And yet,

Hollie had taken life with both hands and done something truly incredible with herself.

And so have you, Matthews.

It took reminding, but he was getting there.

"I just...I'm leaving again." Her voice was soft by firm. "I'm not going to stand here and lie to you and say the other night was some big mistake. It complicates the living hell of out things, but I don't regret it." She paused, and had there ever been so weighted a quiet space in his life? "But I'm not staying. Wolf Creek" — she seemed to struggle — "Wolf Creek isn't my home anymore. And I need to put the cards on the table from the start."

Sawyer was quiet for a long moment, absorbing the things she had said. He hadn't ever expected her to stay. Fool him twice and the naivety of youth would have been at play there. But that she was so open about her plans to leave, with all the unfinished business and the way they were together? It made him forget the anger, if temporarily, and replace it with something...sad.

"So what, then?" he asked. "We screw your brains out once and shake hands and leave it at that for the rest of our lives?"

She winced and Sawyer realized it wasn't because of his intentionally crude words.

"You've seen Easton again, haven't you?" he asked, doing his best to keep the rising anger well below the tide line. "When, today? I think I deserve that much truth from you, at least."

"Yes, for fuck's sake, I saw Cade yesterday. It is my *job* to speak to Cade — and you, I might add. And things progressed from there. I don't need to go about reporting on my every move to you, thank you very much, Captain."

"So what then?" Sawyer asked. "Tell me what you're looking for here, Hollie, because I'm lost."

"So am I, Sawyer." That came out loud, nearly a yell, and it paused him in mid-speech. "I don't know what I'm supposed to be doing here, okay? I came back to do a job and it seems like I can't keep my head straight around either you or Cade long enough to do that. There is some obvious and complicated history between us, Lord above knows it, but whenever I am around *either* of you, all I can think about is stripping you down and having my way with your naked body and that *terrifies* me. So you tell me. So what?"

Sawyer looked as though he had been about to say something, about to refute her argument or push the matter further, but he stopped before he started and simply looked at her, a wild, intense desire radiating from those deep green eyes, his freckles dancing when he arched one thick eyebrow and parted his lips. The small movement was enough to make Hollie's body ache for him, to make her want things she really shouldn't want, let alone have.

But why not?

She hadn't left Cade's office the previous day feeling any worse than she had for having slept with both of them the night before. Why couldn't she have Sawyer right here in the firehouse bunker? He was already half-undressed and looking at her if he was so, so hungry and Hollie didn't know how to handle that expression with anything other than a 'yes please, sailor.'

"You're playing with fire, Hollyhock," he muttered, low and guttural, taking another step toward her, which had Hollie's back up against the wall and her bag slipping from her shoulders and landing on the ground.

"Good thing you're a firefighter, then," she murmured, though God, that barely sounded like her voice, not with the husky tinge and the extra breathiness.

"But, darlin'..." He was towering over her now, and had Hollie truly ever been so aware of a man before in her life, what with his bulk and his straining muscles and that expression in his eye that promised, promised, promised? "I'm the fire you're playing with."

God, he was. Because when he bent down and captured her lips with his mouth, Hollie didn't hesitate, didn't protest. She simply gave herself fully over to him, allowed Sawyer to be the next extreme jump she took, the next mountain she climbed...

Interesting turn of phrase.

But, then again, she did have every intention of climbing the man like a tree and there was no use denying it to herself. Instead, she simply pressed back against the kiss and Sawyer's big, powerful body, sliding her leg up the side of his muscled flank until she was drawing him as close to her body and her throbbing center as she could. It hardly made sense that she was still so aroused, so easily turned to needy, pulsating lust after all the delicious experiences she'd enjoyed over the last few days, but there was something about this man and the way he stripped down her defenses and made her feel like she could truly be herself again that had her opening up and letting him in.

And hopefully in more ways than one.

"Bed," he murmured.

Hollie just gave her head a shake. "Here is fine," she managed, barely. Her entire body was on fire and she ached for more of his touch, for the way his thick beard felt against her skin, for how she would undoubtedly yield to him when he parted her legs and…

One of his calloused hands found her nipple through the fabric of her shirt and twisted slightly, making Hollie moan and writhe at his touch. She unzipped her jacket as quickly as she could and tossed it off to the side, working alongside Sawyer's rough movements to pull her shirt free as well.

Her bra was a light green number — simple but pretty and if the way Sawyer looked at her in it was any indication, he wholeheartedly approved. The more important matter was getting them both out of their jeans as quickly as possible.

But Sawyer was making that challenging, because he wasn't just turning her mind to a puddle of desire, but also nuzzling soft, sweet kisses against her neck and her collarbone and the swells of her breasts and, *God*, it made it hard to think about anything else. He dipped his head into the valley and slid his tongue across her sensitive flesh, and Hollie bucked into his touch and brought her hands up to pull at his long, soft hair. He groaned at the movement and she did it again, then scraped her nails across the nape of his neck, which made a guttural sound tear from the back of his throat.

"Hollie…" His tone was thick and right on the edge, and she loved how it made her feel, how it caught up in her belly and sent shivers of anticipation racing up her spine.

"I want you." It was the only thing that she could manage, the only truth that mattered in those moments, and she focused on it, on getting the rest of their clothing off so that he could fill her body like his eyes and lips kept promising he was going to do.

But still, Sawyer kept his slow, relentlessly controlled pace and it was almost something to marvel at, that this hulking, handsome brute of a man was so very gentle and very soft, and Hollie was sure there was something behind it, the calming of the beast, but she was far too wrapped up in wanting more of his touch to dive into psych 101 at the moment.

"Please, Sawyer."

It must have been the *please* that did it, because his movements quickened and he started on the button of her jeans, then made quick work of the zipper and pulling her pants and panties down her legs, pausing to squeeze her ass in a rough, delicious movement that made Hollie suck in a breath. She slipped out of her boots and Sawyer pulled her jeans and socks off until she stood in the Wolf Creek Firehouse bunker wearing only her bra.

And the heat of Sawyer's gaze upon her.

He placed one thick hand on the wall above her head and leaned down to growl in her ear.

"I want to take you slow and long," he said. "But fuck, if I can't wait to have you, Hollie."

Her chest was rising and falling rapidly now and Hollie could barely control her thoughts, let alone her actions.

"Have me," she said, "God, please have me."

He unzipped his own jeans and let them fall to the floor then quickly pulled his thick, hard cock free of his briefs. God, he was big. The other night he had been big in her mouth, but now Hollie ached for him to fill her, to stretch her body like she had never felt before.

He pulled a condom from his back pocket and she was so relieved that he'd thought to prepare that she didn't even comment on his expectation of needing one at hand. In another moment, his throbbing cock was sheathed and he was at her entrance, pressing that hardness into her wet heat and making Hollie suck in a breath. She wanted him. God, she wanted him with the kind of intensity she barely understood. She couldn't think, but she could act and she moved on instinct to wrap her legs around him so it was just Sawyer's powerful muscles holding her against the wall. Then slowly—God, it felt so fucking slow—he began to lower her down onto his cock.

Hollie sucked in a tight breath. He was big and beautiful and each inch filled her more, forced her body to blissfully accommodate his size. She wrapped her arms around his neck and pulled him in for a blistering kiss, loving the scrape of his beard against her skin and each extra inch he plunged into her.

"Fuck, Hol." His voice was practically animalistic. "You feel so fucking good, baby." She couldn't think to respond, merely wrapped his long hair in her hand and pulled, scraping her nails up and down his neck, demanding and promising without words.

He sank the last bit of himself into her and Hollie bit down on his neck to keep from screaming loud enough for the whole town to hear. Distantly, she remembered that they were in an open bunker, that his team could come back at any moment and get quite the show, but she didn't actually care. All she cared about was the slide of his cock in and out of her pussy, how safe she felt with his body wrapped around hers, the delicious press of his strong, muscled legs against her ass as he supported and filled her.

Sawyer had always supported her. He had been a place she could turn to growing up when no one else would understand. Cade had been her coming home. Sawyer had been her quest for adventure. The two of them, separately but at the same time, had been all she had needed to realize her true self, and she was finding this out far, far too late.

Or rather, she was giving in to it far too late, with every rough thrust and gentle slide, and her pulse began to rachet up, especially when he brought one hand down to where their bodies connected and stroked her clit, making her arch up into him and allowing his cock even deeper into her pussy.

"Sawyer." She managed to moan his name, guttural and unrecognizable as her own voice.

"That's right, baby," he murmured. "Come for me, Hollie. Come all over my cock. I wanna feel your pussy tighten around me." He had every capacity to be gentle, just as he had every capacity to be rough and domineering, and Hollie couldn't say for certain which version she liked more.

Then he pinched her clit.

She hadn't been expecting it and the explosion of pain and pleasure sent her careening toward the edge of the cliff, falling hard and fast over the side into an abyss of beautiful, delicious sensation. She rocked against him hard, once, twice, once more, riding out the releases until her breath was coming in rough pants and her whole body was alive with electricity and need.

"Again, Hollie."

Hollie barely registered the words, but after a moment she looked up at him, up at those dark, rough eyes promising oh so much more pleasure if she could just trust him. Her instinct kicked in and she wrapped him back up in her arms and pulled him as close to her body as she could, scraping his bare skin with her nails, pulling his hair in rough tugs and demanding with everything she had that he come with her this time, that he fall right off the edge by her side into shared wildness and freedom.

Sawyer was beginning to lose control too. She could feel it, so took the lead, giving as much to Sawyer as he gave to her, until her own release seemed impossible to ignore and she felt the intensity taking over her body until one, two, three more thrusts and she was losing the ground beneath her and the wall against her back, until she was releasing a string of curses and praises and his name. He surged and pumped hard, giving over to her as she had done to him until they were both riding their waves of beautiful, overwhelming pleasure.

Slowly, Sawyer released her legs and let her back down to the ground. He pulled the condom off and disappeared for a moment, returned with a soft, warm cloth which he used to gently clean her skin. It was almost difficult to reconcile this enormous, powerful, fearless man with such kind and gentle caresses, but there something so innate about it, as if the whole universe came together when he brushed her skin with featherlight touches.

After all they had just shared, after all the wounds they'd opened upon her arrival home and her arrival at the fire station, Hollie didn't like the silence stretching between them. She wanted more, wanted more of the conversation — damning as it had been for her — wanted more of the confessions and the intimacy they had once shared. She wanted it all back.

But not just with Sawyer.

Which left her in exactly the same place she had been the day she'd packed up and left Wolf Creek on the night of their graduation.

"Sawyer," she said quietly. He looked up and met her gaze and goodness, those dark green eyes were expressive and beautiful — even more so than she had remembered them to be. "Is there ever a chance you'll forgive me for leaving?" Hollie hadn't realized that was the question she was planning on asking until it was out of her mouth, but here she was and there was no going back.

Sawyer's expression was sad and Hollie knew she would do just about anything to make him smile, to put that rough, happy grin back on his face, rare as it was. He was a brute on the outside, there was no denying that, a self-built shell to keep out so much of what life had already thrown at him, but he had let her in once — and it gave her hope.

"You hurt me, Hollie," he said. "Not by leaving. I wish you hadn't left, but I know you and I know that you had to go. But come on." He shook his head and those soft, beautiful red curls practically danced across his shoulders. "You didn't say a word. You didn't trust me enough to tell me anything before you left. What was I supposed to think?"

"I...I wouldn't have gone," she said, in a tone so low it could only be called a confession. "If I had stayed and told either of you that I was leaving...I wouldn't have left."

Sawyer did smile this time, but it almost broke her heart.

"What would have been so awful about that?"

Chapter Twelve

There was absolutely no denying that Cam and Savannah were making a concerted effort not to look at each other. Hollie knew that because she was watching the two of them while she made her own concerted effort not to look at either Cade or Sawyer, or even Lily or Maddy Hollis, since both women seemed to have her number and she was pretty sure they had filled in all the missing pieces, which really managed to freak her out.

Okay, maybe it wasn't so much that they knew that was making Hollie freak out. It was that there was anything *to* know. She had been assigned to do a job in this ridiculous memory box of a town and all she had managed was the one thing she had promised herself she wouldn't. *Rather, the two things.*

But it wasn't just about sex. It hadn't been just about sex the night she had fled town and it certainly wasn't just about sex now. Hell, it would have been so much easier if it were just about sex, and not the way Cade and Sawyer both made her feel like she was living in high definition, like she was taking the greatest adventure of her life but a comfy, cozy home would always be warm and waiting for her when she returned. And what the hell and damnation was she supposed to do about that? Because her fear of falling for both these men had driven her away in the first place and she had come back to find that there was a pretty obvious reason she hadn't found love in the years since.

Love.

No one was talking about love.

"All I'm saying, Chief, is that if your men had been on the ground..."

She had been so lost in thought that she hadn't even realized Cade and Sawyer were bickering at the far end of the table and, by the looks of it, things were intensifying by the moment. Undoubtedly, her presence and subsequent behavior here had only made the relationship between the two men all more the challenging.

"Aye." This from Christian, who had just walked through the door with Ryder on his heels. "I don't give a shit if you're the sheriff, fire captain or the Queen of England," he said. "We have an emergency situation about to bite us in the ass and if you two can't get your shit together, we'll figure it out without you."

It was the most amount of words she'd heard Christian Harlow say in maybe ever, but Hollie had to give him credit for using them when it mattered.

"Thank you, Christian," she said, standing up at the head of the table and walking to the front of the room. "Now, wind speeds are expected to increase tonight, so we can anticipate losing more trees and pretty much assume the power will be out for the next week. The broadcasts have been effective, the town is stocked up on water and food, and we've shared our emergency preparations lists. So far, we're not issuing a mandatory evacuation notice, but we've seen some movement near the bridge, so it looks like residents are leaving of their own accord. Revised maps show zones two, four and five are in the direct path of the flooding. Protecting the reservoir and keeping the bridge clear in those areas are our main focuses."

They finalized their plans, marking iPads and notebooks. The tone of the room grew more tense with every passing moment. Weather reports were often wrong—hell, if anyone knew that, it was Hollie. In her field, expecting something to be wrong came with the territory. But the storms had been coming harder and faster all week and there was little doubt in her mind or anyone else's that whatever flooding was expected would arrive shortly.

She chanced a look out of the window of the lounge at the Black Reef Mountains in the near distance. They were topped with white and great, dark stone and trees peeking out from snowcaps that were promising to melt and career down the mountain in, supposedly, the next twelve to twenty-four hours.

"Are your homes all secure for the storm?" she asked those at the table, glancing to Dec, Micah and Lily, Maddy, Camilla and finally, Cade and Sawyer, who, inexplicably, were still sitting next to each other, as if it were preferable to poke at each other rather than to remove themselves from the situation.

"Cabin's at the ridgeline," Dec explained. "We'll probably get tree damage, but we won't get flooding." As it was, he and Micah were two of the most capable survival experts in the country and she would likely need their advice before this was all over.

"We've got the B&B boarded and the cabins secured," Maddy said, "Yours and Savannah's have both been sandbagged and I've placed emergency kits inside too." She gave a slight smile. "Not that I'm expecting either of you are going to be resting anytime in the near future."

Hollie smiled in return. Maddy was the kind of person who'd just integrated herself into her life without the messy getting-to-know-you. In fact, Hollie felt a little as though she had known both Hollis sisters for years, which was particularly laughable, given that she'd hardly known anyone for years except for a handful of the people in this room.

"Cam," she asked, turning her attention back to the matter at hand, "is your house secured for flooding?"

Camilla nodded. "We've got the sump pump in the yard and the windows covered."

Before she could get to either Cade or Sawyer, Cade spoke up.

"Hollie, we're all fine. You've prepared the whole town for a worst-case scenario and we're ready because of you, okay?"

God, but his voice made her feel like it *was* all going to be okay, like she didn't have thousands of people relying on her to keep them safe, like so much couldn't possibly go wrong. Cade had that uncanny ability to give her the strength she needed to not hold up the world all on her own, and it wasn't just because he was a dominant, capable man. In fact, the dominance was a side effect of who he was at his core, rather than the other way around.

Before she could respond, however, her phone went off, and Hollie excused herself and ducked outside to take Debra Lewitt's call.

"T-minus 12 hours," Hollie said. "I've got sandbag barriers, sump pumps and evacuation plans ready to go."

"Good, Callihan," Debra replied. "Not that I doubted your ability." Hollie went off a quick rundown of the preparations and promised to be in touch when the flooding began, with regular updates on damage control and resources. With questions answered and plans finalized, Lewitt hung up and Hollie slid the phone into the pocket of her windbreaker.

She glanced out to the mountains and spied a small bench at the edge of the path. A few more minutes in the cool quiet air might be what she needed to prepare her mind, body and soul for the day ahead. And it promised to be quite a day — or week — ahead of them.

And yet, for all her professionalism and capability, for all that she loved her job and wanted to do the very best she could, there was that niggling sense of something unresolved, of incomplete business between her and Cade and Sawyer that Hollie couldn't stop thinking about, and their behavior today had only increased her concern. The storms would come and they would go, and when the water receded, she would go too.

Because she had to, right? Because she had to return to the life she had carved for herself, because there was nothing here for her in Wolf Creek, not in the long run.

And yet, how could Hollie deny the beauty of the Black Reef Mountain Range stretching out before her? How could she pretend the fresh air didn't call to something base and memorable, days spent by the lakes, nights under the stars, camping, hiking, climbing? These open woods and mountain ranges had raised her just as surely as her gram had, and there was something truly bittersweet about being back here.

And the men who still called it home.

She felt like a dog chasing her tail. This was the same conversation she'd had with herself years ago, as the truth of her feelings had become more dangerous and difficult to ignore. And she'd broken the one rule she had set out for herself upon returning to this town. But honestly, what had she expected? These things weren't supposed to last.

"Hollie..."

She been so wrapped up in her own thoughts that Hollie hadn't even realized Dec was sitting next to her until he gave her a shove with his elbow. He was just like Wes in that, loving and affectionate and around when she needed him. Well, Wes hadn't been around in a good long time, but it wasn't as though Hollie had needed him...

"You seemed distracted this morning," he said, his voice dropping into a not-quite-whisper, even though they were quite alone on the mountain top outside of the dining hall and the wind was already starting to pick up. "Is everything okay?"

Dec McCormick played a good game, he always had. He'd tried his charms on her a time or two, but though he was incredibly handsome, there had never been that spark. She was grateful for it. Not succumbing to Dec's charms meant she had gotten to know the man underneath, and he was kind, open and willing to go to battle for those he loved.

"I don't know what you're talking about," Hollie replied, because though he was a good man, she didn't need to bring Dec or Micah or Lily or any of them into this complicated mess of things.

"I'm sure you don't," he replied. "But since you weren't distracted, perhaps you might have some insight into why the chief and the sheriff nearly came to blows this morning."

Hollie turned to him and raised an eyebrow.

"I'm not certain I like your implication, Deckard," she said. He shot her the same look Wes had a thousand times when she had called him Westland.

"Fine then," he replied. "I'll be blunter. Those two have been sniping for years, but when you came to town, things got even worse." The look on his face said he wasn't asking questions he already knew the answers to. "You've been distracted, more so than I've ever seen you on a job, and you're not making eye contact with anyone who might have some idea how you're feeling." He wrapped his arm around her shoulder and pulled her in for a side hug.

"Now, Hollie, I may not be a smart man..." She made to protest, but he continued, "but I have to say that seems rather foolish, considering there are plenty of folks in a twenty-foot radius who happen to have a good idea of what you're going through and some concept of what to do next."

"It's not going to work."

She blurted it out almost before Dec had finished talking and he pulled back to give her a smug smile that Hollie had half a mind to wipe off his face. She was still an unrefined dirt child from the wilds of Montana, after all.

"Why not?' he asked. "And do you even really know what you don't want to work, or are you cutting out all possibility because you're terrified, without even looking at your options?"

"How did things go down with Lily?" she asked. "Because I guarantee it wasn't the result of a decade of radio silence, broken trust and mutual dislike."

"You're right," Dec replied. "Things are complicated with you — that's valid and I won't argue it. But things were complicated with Lily and Micah and me too. Things were complicated with Aubrey." Hollie winced at the reminder of the woman who had broken Dec's heart the year before. "Things will always be complicated where love is concerned, no matter what kind of love that is. But." He paused and gave her a very pointed look. "Love is worth fighting for. It's worth being vulnerable for and it's worth giving in to." The expression in his eyes made Hollie actually believe in true love, which was a thing and a half if she were being honest.

"They hate each other," she said quietly, voicing her deepest concerns out loud. "They've been fighting for years and I don't even really know why and even if something could happen, that would make things really hard for us."

She hadn't actually considered an *us*, an us in anything other than the abstract, not in the reality of her somehow forging a relationship the likes of which Dec enjoyed every day.

"They don't hate each other," Dec replied. "They blame each other, but they don't hate each other."

"So what?" It was somehow both a massive relief to talk about this and one of the most terrifying conversations she had ever had, because Dec made it sound real — not easy, not without its challenges — but real, as though she could simply decide that she was going to go ahead and follow this wild and crazy path, and that everyone else would just be on board with it.

"Hollie, do you have feelings for Cade and Sawyer?" he asked simply.

She didn't say anything for a moment. Saying it out loud would make it final, would give it concrete form that made it impossible to ignore. Saying it out loud would mean she had some very important decisions to make in the next days when she was supposed to be focusing on saving lives.

"We slept together," she said, instead. "Once together-together...then...well, once at the fire department and once at the police station."

Dec was making an obvious effort not to laugh in her face and she cut him a dark glance. He held his hands up in surrender and finally gave over to the giggles.

"I know you slept together," he said. "Even if the totally hot expressions you all keep shooting each other when you think no one's looking didn't give it away — which they totally do—you left your panties in the lounge the other day. Not exactly subtle."

Hollie dropped her headed into her hands and let out a low groan.

"Does everyone know?" she asked through her fingers. Not that it mattered. Once she left Wolf Creek, she would never see any of these people again.

A thought that left her surprisingly sad.

Beside her, Declan gave a shrug. "We're not blind, Hol. There's obviously something going on between the three of you and, well, we're pretty good at recognizing the signs." He paused. "But that's not what I asked. I asked if you had feelings for them, and judging by the fact that you changed the conversation, I have my answer."

"It's complicated," she repeated, still with her hands over her head.

"So you've said," Dec replied. And it was interesting to see him this way, the man who had been a carefree flirt to cover up hidden hurts from his past, suddenly a sage on love and ready to dispense wisdom to willing and reluctant souls alike.

They were quiet for a moment and Hollie watched the birds swoop low and dark against a bright white sky. In another week or so, the whole mountain would be lush with colors — bursting greens, patches of blue and yellow wildflowers as far as the eye could see, pink and orange. She wasn't above admitting that she'd missed the sight, that of all the beauties she had visited across the world, there was something extra special about Wolf Creek in the spring.

"Yes," she said quietly, pulling her hands away from her face to look Dec in the eye. "Yes, I have feelings for them, both of them, and I'm confused and scared and not sure what to do next."

Dec took her hand in his, and it was a comfort that made her want to call Wes when she got home. Once the storm was over. *And the natural disaster too.*

"You talk to them, Hollie. You take that leap you've always been the first to take and you allow yourself to be vulnerable."

"What if I get hurt?" she said, saying it out loud for the first time. "What if I hurt them?"

Dec placed a chaste kiss on her head and stood.

"What if you don't?"

Chapter Thirteen

Sawyer caught up with Cade just as he was walking back from his Bronco. Cade had just pocketed his cell phone and looked as though he wanted any excuse in the world not to talk.

"She's going to leave after this storm passes," Sawyer said without preamble. "And there's nothing either of us can do about it on our own."

The expression on Cade's face told Sawyer he had come to the same conclusion.

"What do you suggest?" Cade asked. "Hollie's never done anything she didn't want to do and if she wanted to stay, she would."

"We haven't given her any reason to stay," Sawyer replied, and it made his chest feel a little tight. They hadn't given her any reason to stay beyond spectacular lovemaking against walls, tables and floors. "I know she slept with you. And for right now, it's not what I'm worried about." Was that actual admiration in Cade's gaze? Sawyer wasn't entirely sure what to make of it.

"I think we have to talk to her," Cade said quietly, as if the idea of the two of them going to do anything together was unfathomable, despite all that had happened between them in the last few days, and despite the incredible communication they had shared that night they had seduced Hollie, without a word, without asking each other for permission.

"She's back in her cabin right now," Sawyer replied. "Savannah told her to go sleep before the calls came in. Might be the last chance we get."

And he hated that he had to ask for Cade's help the same way that he hated that Cade was involved at all, but the draw he felt for the woman who had torn his heart out when they'd been nothing more than kids was so much stronger. If it was a matter of talking to her with Cade Easton at his side or not talking to her at all, Sawyer knew which option he would pick.

"This doesn't mean we're friends," Cade replied grudgingly, but they started down the path toward her cabin together. There was a light on in her room and since Savannah, the only other resident of the Triple Diamond B&B at the moment, was still safely up in the lodge, there was no second-guessing where to go. They walked in silence, but Sawyer had to admit that the undercurrent of tension that had long existed between the two of them was almost a comfort. With everything else on its head the second Hollie had walked into town with her pretty lips, luscious ass and adventurous spirit that made the world around her sit up and take notice, Sawyer was almost grateful for that reminder that some things never changed.

Though, of course, they could. The bridge between him and Cade Easton wasn't exactly impassable. They'd never been best friends. In fact, Sawyer had really only had one best friend until joining the fire department, and she had skipped town the moment things had gotten rough. But the deep, abiding dislike between them had, once, stemmed from a place of hurt and sadness.

A place of love.

Sawyer wanted to punch himself in the face for even thinking it. But once the idea had taken root, it was almost difficult to ignore. Hollie had left them both without a word and it had just made them turn on each other, rather than forming some kind of plan to get her to come back. Granted, it had been years in which they had fostered this deep resentment and anger, and that sort of thing didn't just go away, but...

They stopped outside her door and Cade gave him a look Sawyer couldn't even begin to interpret.

"Hol, you home?" he called out. No answer, though movement in the cabin indicated she was awake. Was she avoiding them? He wouldn't have blamed her — hell, he'd probably turn tail and run in the other direction if he were in her shoes.

Which he really hoped she wasn't about to do.

"Hollie." Sawyer's voice was low and rough and he knew that he could get used to saying her name every day for the rest of his life.

"Sheriff, you want to do the honors?" Sawyer asked, with only some of his usual sarcasm. Cade didn't even comment on it. *Strange times for us both, it seems.*

"Hollie." Cade pushed open the door to the cabin and called her name when they walked inside. Maddy Hollis had done one hell of a job decorating the place, Sawyer had to admit. It was homey and rustic, like the front of a Hallmark card or something just as schlocky, but it didn't feel forced. It felt genuine, like coming home.

Like seeing Hollie Callihan again.

There was movement in the bedroom and Sawyer followed Cade down the hallway until the two of them came to an abrupt stop. Hollie was in a pair of shorts and a light pink bra. Headphones peeked out from until her lush piles of blonde curls, which he rarely saw down, and she was swinging her hips and dancing as if she didn't have a care in the world.

And oh, *shit*, Hollie could dance. The way she moved her ass reminded Sawyer of exactly what it had felt like to have that ass in his hands as she arched against him, as they gave over to each other against the wall at the fire station. Her body was smooth and lithe and muscled and he wanted to lick her all over, to give in to this maddening lust for this woman every single day for the rest of their lives.

"Hollie," Sawyer tried again, but she must have been wearing noise-resistant headphones, because she still didn't turn around. Cade stepped forward and made an obvious effort to be gentle about getting her attention, but she was so lost in her own world that the moment he touched her she let out a screech and yanked the headphones from her ears.

"Jesus *Christ*," she said, placing her hand to her chest, which Sawyer had difficultly not watching fluttering up and down. He'd held her breasts in his hands. He'd caressed the swollen nipples pushing at the cotton of her bra and he'd pressed his mouth to the hot apex of her thighs until she had screamed his name, pulled his hair and come hard against his tongue. He very much understood the idea of tasting the forbidden fruit now.

"Sorry, Hol," Cade said, "we called your name a few times, but you didn't hear us." She gave him a look that Sawyer took to interpret as *I know you're right, but I don't need to be happy about it.*

"What are you guys doing here?" she asked. "We should all get some rest before the party starts." She wasn't wrong, but the idea of letting her walk away without even having the conversation was enough to make Sawyer feel caged and claustrophobic. He didn't understand it—hell, he wasn't even sure he wanted to understand it. He had cared so much for the girl and she had gone and broken his heart. It would be foolish, then, to care so much for the woman with the same power.

"We need to talk," he said gruffly. "And we know you're going to try to pull a Houdini on us the moment the storms settle, so we're doing it now." Some things hadn't changed, and the expression in Hollie's eyes gave him all the insight he needed to know that he had been right about her intentions to pull a disappearing trick.

"I don't know what you're talking about."

"Of course not," Cade replied. "In fact, you were planning to seek us out and tell us everything and discuss all of your feeling and emotions, then give us the chance to share ours, right?" Hollie looked like an angry pixie, which Sawyer did not point out.

"How do you know I wasn't?" she asked, then winced, as if just remembering how everything had gone down the last time. "Fine, you're right. Talk, then. Come on."

"Can you put on a shirt first?" Sawyer asked, pointedly dropping his gaze to her still heaving chest. "I can't concentrate right now."

"Always the caveman," Cade sniped.

Sawyer elbowed him in the ribs and got a very satisfying puff of air from Cade's parted lips in return.

"Least I know how to keep a woman in my cave so she doesn't go wandering," he replied. "Would you like some tips?"

Hollie had gone off in search of a shirt, which Sawyer had to note was a flimsy tank top that only cupped her breasts and made him wants to trace the peaks of nipples that showed through the fabric. Then again, Hollie could have been wearing a bag and he would still have ached to touch her again—the FEMA windbreaker had been proof enough of that. She led them out of her bedroom and into the living room before the fire, where she perched on a chair and indicated for the two of them to sit on the sofa like errant schoolboys. He hadn't considered the kink before, but if Hollie was his teacher, he certainly wouldn't rule it out.

"You wanted to talk," she said, darting her gaze between the two of them. "So talk."

"This was your brilliant idea," Cade mumbled.

"Not my fault you can't string two words together," Sawyer replied instinctively. They'd been fighting like this for years and all those old hurts were right back at the surface, threatening to send her so far away she never came back—not even for a natural disaster.

"What?" She stopped her nervous fidgeting and crossed her arms over her chest. "What the hell is it between you two? The only time you've agreed on anything since I came back was when you were tearing off my clothes on the table in the lodge, which"—she took a moment to point at them both—"everyone apparently knows about." This was news to Sawyer, but not very important news. Which was good because Hollie was back to giving them both the look that somehow made Sawyer feet contrite and aroused at the same time.

"I know you weren't the best of friends, but for fuck's sake, if this is all because of me…" She came up short and rolled her head back until it rested against the wall behind her. "This is because of me."

It wasn't a question.

"Hollie." Sawyer walked over to her, drawn to her conflict and challenging beauty even more now than he had ever been, desperate to make her see… See what? That they could be together, that somehow this insane relationship between them had a happy ending? There wasn't a snowball's chance in hell of that. It worked fine for Dec and Micah and it worked fine for Christian and Ryder too, but those men were friends, family to each other. Communication and trust came naturally to their relationships in a way he and Cade would never share.

Not that he had any plans of sharing.

And yet.

"We didn't know why you ran away," Cade explained, sitting on the edge of the couch and crossing his arms over his chest. "We didn't know how you felt. We just both thought we had done something wrong."

Apparently, they *had* done something wrong, hadn't shown her a willingness to be open for discussion, hadn't made her feel safe enough to share her secret. "We were young and both…" He shook his head and a part of Sawyer—not one he was entirely proud of— took a small amount of pleasure in the fact that Cade Easton didn't always know the exact right thing to say. "We were both angry, Hollie. You knew our lives better than anyone. You knew that no one stuck around for kids like us, no one ever looked back when they drove away." There was no denying the note of pain in Cade's voice and Sawyer knew their paths ran a tangled parallel even without Hollie's homecoming.

"I wasn't leaving you." God, if this woman started to cry Sawyer was cooked as a Thanksgiving turkey. He'd seen Hollie cry only a handful of times in their shared years and it had almost brought him to his knees every time. "I was protecting you." She raked her hand through her hair and gave an exasperated sigh. "It wasn't just that I wanted you both," she said quietly. "God only knows how much I wanted you." This followed by a self-aware laugh that had Sawyer thinking about the firehouse bunker wall and the table in the lodge. "But it wasn't just that."

She stood up and start pacing in front of the fireplace, her movements hurried and fidgety. Then she stopped and looked him directly in the eye.

"I had feelings for you both," she said, her voice calm and firm, as if she were acknowledging this truth for the first time out loud and it was somehow freeing her. Sawyer could understand that. "I had feelings for you both and I was terrified. Wes was gone, Gram was gone and I was falling in love with my two best friends. What would you have done?"

She tore her gaze from him and turned to Cade, who was looking at her in a way Sawyer had never seen before—and he'd been all too aware of the way Cade had always looked at her. Their relationship had been one of amicable distance, an understanding that Hollie had room in her life for them both and raising a fuss would only make her unhappy. They disagreed a lot, but he and Cade had both always done their best to make sure Hollie was happy.

How would love be any different from friendship?

But love *was* different and Sawyer didn't see any way around that.

"Hollie, darlin', you could have trusted us." Cade was using his *put down the gun* voice and Sawyer wasn't sure which of them it was for.

"Honestly, what would you have said?" She directed her question first at Cade, then at Sawyer who gave his head a slight shake.

"I don't know," he replied honestly. "But I wouldn't have been sitting around for eight years wondering why I wasn't good enough for an explanation, Hol. At least I would have known why." This followed by a laugh. "And hell, who knows what might have happened down at the lake that night if you had said something." Out of the corner of his eye, Sawyer saw Cade's eyebrow raise. Then a smirk spread across his lips.

"I have some idea," Cade said. And just like that, the tone of the room changed. There was no light chill from the spring air, no coldness from the conversation.

It was just three of them, with their fucked-up past and their intense desires.

"I think I have some idea too," Sawyer added, catching Hollie's gaze and giving her a wink. "Question is, Callihan, what would you have done about it?"

Chapter Fourteen

When did it get so fucking hot in this cabin? She was wearing loose cotton shorts and a tank top, the sleepwear she'd been planning to crash in for a few hours before go-time, when Sawyer and Cade had walked right into her room and made themselves at home. And made the place feel a damn sight smaller with their massive presences. Or maybe it was just that she was overwhelmed by them, by everything they were offering, by the promises in twin green and brown eyes.

"I don't know," she said. A lie and they both knew it, if the intensity in their gazes was anything to go.

"Try again, Hollyhock," Cade replied. "What do you think would have happened down at the lake that night if you had told us what you wanted? Do you think we would have all gone home and gone to bed?"

Memories of the night at the lake came back to her, of the three of them under the stars, sharing a bottle of sherry she had found tucked in the back of a liquor cabinet she'd sold after the will had been read. The night had been warm and they'd been fresh graduates of Lewis and Clark County High School, eighteen years old and ready to take on the world.

"Or, Hollie," Sawyer continued where Cade had left off, "would you have admitted what you just told us, would you have confessed to wanting something tawdry and base right there at the riverbank?"

It was her turn to follow the thread of the story and so she did, not giving into her fear of what might come next, not this time.

"I would have confessed to wanting you both," she said, her voice coming out on a breath. "Then I would have tried to escape, to jump in the lake or something."

"Would we have let you go?" Cade asked, coming to stand behind her, to wrap one arm around her waist and whisper in her ear. She shook her head.

"No." This was barely a word. "No, you would have wrestled me or tickled me or something." He brought his hand to her upper ribs and caressed her through the fabric of her tank top until she was writhing in his arms. Cade let out a deep groan and Hollie grinned.

"You're being a tease," Sawyer observed from his perch against the wall in front of her. "Poor sheriff's going to cream his pants pretty soon if you keep rubbing your pretty little ass up against him."

"And what about you?" she replied, rubbing her pretty little ass up against Cade's erection, and held Sawyer's gaze. "You'd have pulled me into your lap, right? Then tortured my neck and back with kisses while Cade ran his hands up my leg."

Cade ran his hands up her leg.

"Just your neck and back, Hollie?" Sawyer asked. "Because you seemed to enjoy it quite a bit when I ate your sweet pussy while you were spread out on the table. I think you'd be begging me something sweet to do it to you under the stars."

Her breath hitched and she nodded. "Yes." It seemed to be about the only word she could manage at the moment.

"Would you have let us fuck you that night, Hollyhock?" Cade whispered in her ear, then trailed his tongue over the curve of her neck until she was practically shaking in his arms. When Sawyer pushed off the wall and came to stand in front of her, the support was necessary since her knees were starting to give way.

"Would you have given over to both of us for the night, opened your body and heart to us?"

Sawyer had one hand on her ass and the other hand rounding the curve of her breast and playing none-too-gently with her nipple. Cade was trailing those damning kisses along her skin, making her swear and buck and ache for him. This teasing was driving her absolutely insane.

"More."

By unspoken agreement, the movements against her skin and nipples and throat stopped.

"Did you want it?" Cade asked. "That night, did you want it?"

She nodded desperately.

"And right now, Hollie, do you want it? Both of us, taking you over and over again until you forget your name? Tell us."

"Fuck me." It was barely audible.

"Try again, baby," Sawyer replied. "We want to hear you."

"I need you both to fuck me," she said. "Now."

That was all it took—Sawyer had her up and over his shoulder in one swift movement, and Hollie would have protested, but there was no denying how fucking hot it was that he could just throw her over his shoulder and carry her into the bedroom, Cade right behind them, his gaze making her feel hot and needy all over again.

Sawyer placed her on the bed and wasted no time yanking her shorts down and spreading her legs wide. He was, at the heart of it, a rough-and-tumble man, who made her come hard with gentle words and strong movements.

"Touch yourself," Cade said, leaning against the doorframe in his Dom pose—a pose she was coming to love and hate all at the same time. "I want to see you rub your pretty pink nipples while Sawyer makes you scream."

Hollie didn't have it in her to protest and she went to push her bra off, but Sawyer was there, making quick work of it until she was bare save for a pair of silver panties.

She was quickly losing her mind to lust and desire, but that didn't need to mean she had to go down alone, so Hollie made a show of sliding two fingers into her mouth and sucking hard and deep before she brought them down to her nipple and slowly—*God, so slowly*—began to circle the tight, peaked bud.

"You want more, kitten?" Cade asked. "Go harder, give yourself what you really want."

What she really wanted was... *Too much, too rough and too debauched, surely not...*

"I know you want more," Cade said. "What exactly is it?"

"It's nothing..." The lie dripped from every syllable.

Sawyer brought his tongue flat against her slick panties and Hollie almost screamed.

"Trust us, Hollie," he said, sliding one finger past the elastic and pressing it into her.

"It's embarrassing," she moaned, though really, what was left at this point?

Sawyer moved his fingers inside her and she bucked to get more contact. Then he stopped and brought his other hand to her waist so she couldn't force more pressure from his touch.

"Hollie."

She was shaking now, half from nerves about what they might say and half in anticipation that they might actually do it. Well, more than half.

She nodded to the suitcase near the window. "In the pouch, near the top," she said, each word punctuated by a moan when Sawyer flicked his finger against her swollen clit. Cade made slow and agonizing work of finding what she asked for, but she could see the moment he opened the bag.

"My, my, my..." His words felt like caresses. "You haven't lost your adventurous spirit, darlin'."

He brought the bag over to Sawyer, who glanced inside, then back up at her, his eyes hooded with lust and anticipation.

"Tell me you want us to use these," Cade said. "Because the idea of you at our mercy is just about as sexy as it gets, Hollie, because I don't think a day of my life is ever going to go by without the image of you wearing these." He pulled the nipple clamps from the bag and let them dangle from one strong finger. Hollie nodded, needing that spark of pain, needing to feel her skin burn with that primal current of lust and heat.

Cade was at her side in an instant, slowly, gently, placing one clamp, then the other over her straining nipples. The pain came at her all at once, then faded over into a desperate, writhing pleasure that made Hollie see stars behind her closed eyes.

"Sit up, sweet one," Cade said, and Sawyer pulled free of her body so Hollie could sit up and wiggle out of her panties, each jostle sending those same sparks of pleasure through her and making her ache for more. The mattress dipped beside her and she turned to see Sawyer sitting at the head of the bed, waiting for her, his thick cock straining against his briefs. When he'd lost the rest of his clothing, Hollie couldn't be certain. All she knew was that she ached to climb on top of him and ride him all night long.

"Come here," Sawyer said, and Hollie got as far as the elastic of his briefs before she sank down onto her knees and ran her tongue up the length of his cloth-covered cock, until the light fabric was dark and his cock was straining even more to escape. She did it again, reveling in the taste and feel of his hardness and feeling the slick, wet heat of her own desire against her thighs. Every time Sawyer moaned, Hollie's body pulsed around emptiness.

Sawyer, it seemed, couldn't wait and he pushed his briefs off in one rough motion, exposing his hard, thick cock. God, if she didn't get that inside her body soon…

"Ride him, Hollie," Cade said, handing her a condom from her bag. "Ride him."

God, there was just something so intense and sexy about being told what to do, and she quickly got the condom free and down his throbbing cock. Then she was straddling him and slowly, God, so slowly Hollie was sure she would come three times, she lowered herself down upon him.

Sawyer was a big man. Everywhere. Her body stretched to fit him and each inch was an agonizing pleasure that made her wonder if she was even going to survive.

"Put your hands behind your back, sweetheart," Cade murmured against her ear.

She did as she was told and felt the familiar *click* of the bindings pinning her arms against her back. The sensation made her all the more attuned to every touch, every kiss, every brush of Cade's hand across her back and Sawyer's cock deep in her pussy.

"Tell me I'm wrong," Cade murmured and she could hear the sound of his belt coming loose, then his pants and shirt hitting the floor, "but something tells me you want to be filled." Hollie nodded and Cade gave her ass a light tap, heightened by everything else the two men were already doing to her body. "I wasn't done, sweet one." He paused and the silence seemed to stretch on until Hollie was about to give in and beg to know what he was thinking.

"You want to be filled in every hole, don't you, Hollie? You want to have Sawyer pumping into your tight little pussy." He rifled around in the bag behind her and slid a thick dildo across her back, pausing at the valley of her ass cheeks. Hollie couldn't help it—her ass squeezed and Cade and Sawyer both cursed in response.

"You want this in your mouth, Hollie?" he asked. She nodded because she had always loved that aspect of play, that giving up control and responsibility and handing herself entirely over to someone else—someone she trusted.

Two someones she trusted.

Cade handed the pink dildo to Sawyer and he placed it down on the bed to run his finger across her bottom lip.

"You said all her holes, Cade," he practically growled. "Ask her what else she wants before she can't respond anymore." Fuck if those callous, dirty words didn't make Hollie's pussy clench and her swollen nipples throb against the clamps.

"You're going to let me fuck you in the ass," Cade told her as if they didn't already all know it, as if her tight hole wasn't pulsing hard at the idea of feeling him inside her.

"Please..." It was all she could manage with the onslaught of need and sensation these two men were sharing with her with every touch. Cade had clearly found the lube in her bag because a moment later she felt the slick wetness against her hole, and she gasped and pulsed hard around Sawyer.

"God, you're so pretty, all tied up and about to take three cocks at once," Cade muttered, deep and low, as he slowly edged one finger into her ass. Hollie's whole body tightened around him and Cade bent down low to growl into her ear.

"Relax for us, Hollie. We'll make you feel so good."

She knew it and she did relax then, allowing him to slide the second finger into her ass and slowly back out again until she was writhing and bucking against Sawyer's cock and right on the edge.

"Trust me," Cade said and he slowly lined his cock up with her hole. Hollie nodded and felt a surge of protective joy when Cade took one of her bound hands in his and slowly stroked her, bringing calmness and soft pleasures to the hard moment. He pressed into her body.

Hollie knew this part, knew that giving over to the desperation and line of pleasure and pain was the best to enjoy every sensation, every touch and give and take. So she did just that, allowing her body to feel everything all at once until Cade was fully seated in her ass and Sawyer in her pussy.

"Are you okay?" he asked gently, brushing the hair from her head and slowly, oh so slowly, pulling back then pressing back inside her body.

Hollie nodded and let out a low moan.

"Please move, I need..." She wasn't sure what she needed, but they seemed to know because Sawyer had the thick rubber cock at her lips now and Hollie was yielding to it, allowing a third cock inside her as she surrendered to the complete and utter pleasure of the moment. They owned her whole being right then, made her feel safe and protected and understood for all her proclivities and needs, for all the things that made her take chances and leaps of faith.

These men were worth taking a leap of faith on. They were worth asking for more. They were worth telling the truth to.

And she wasn't scared, not anymore, not after how they appreciated her needs and knew them better than she did. How could she be, with this delicious pleasure threatening to overwhelm her?

"Are you going to come for us, Hollie?" Sawyer asked, and brought his thumb to the apex of their connection to rub tight, rough circles across her clit. It was almost too much sensation, but Hollie was able to nod against the onslaught of pleasure.

Until he pinched.

She was flying high and hard before she even realized it, her thoughts chasing themselves with only one idea coming out the victor — pleasure, and desire and bursting heat — and she rode and rode and rode until she could come back to herself and the two men debauching her in all her favorite ways.

"God, you're so fucking pretty when you come," Sawyer half-growled. His hair was loose and curling around his face and Hollie almost wished she could tangle her hands into his hair. "I want to see it again."

It's too soon she wanted to say, too much pleasure, too overwhelming, but the cock in her mouth prevented it and she wasn't entirely certain either man would have taken the step back if she'd said as much. Cade was a Dom by passion and both of them knew her better than she knew herself. Pushing her to heights of pleasure and desire was their main objective.

This was proven by the hard slap Cade landed on her ass in the next moment, which made Hollie buck forward, forcing Sawyer's erection deeper into her cunt. He pressed the cock deeper into her mouth and she accepted willingly, taking it the way she had taken both of these men into her mouth, the way she so loved to do.

"He gave you an order, Hollie," Cade said, bringing his hand back down to slap her ass again, which sent ricochets of pleasure bounding through her body where the two men were connected to her. "It's best you do as you're told."

Except that the intense spanks against her skin were hardly cause to behave when she felt so needy for them, so aching for the sunbursts of pleasure each one brought. She bucked into his touch, sliding slightly away from Sawyer's hard cock, then pressing back down to seat herself fully on top of him. It was all too much, the clamps and the toys and the thick erections filling her up, and each spank sent her so much higher, so much closer to release and redemption, then Cade pulled out of her ass and pushed into her with a roughness that thrilled her and sent her barreling over the edge of pleasure and need. She screamed around the toy in her mouth and rocked between Cade and Sawyer until she merely saw bright spots of beautiful white light behind her eyes and everything felt like bliss and love and burning desire.

When the tremors of her body began to subside, Hollie realized that both men were still hard and throbbing inside her. Mouth still full of the toy, she shook her head, but Sawyer just grinned that dark, lascivious grin that made her nipples tighten and her pussy gush.

"One last time, sweet one," Cade said quietly against the curve of her ear. "Give yourself to us one last time, okay?" When he asked like that, Hollie couldn't even think to deny him, so she nodded slowly and rocked her ravished body into their cocks, each one more swollen and hot and promising of an explosive release.

"So close, baby," Sawyer growled. "I wanna feel you tight around my cock as I come hard in your pretty pussy. Can you do that for me? Can you come hard for me?"

Hollie nodded, suddenly feeling the need to give them both exactly what they wanted as they had given to her. And she was riding in earnest because the waves of her last release had turned into the rising tides of this one and she was pressing back and forth, back and forth until Sawyer brought one hand up to her swollen, tender nipples and gave the clamp a tug.

Hollie couldn't hold on. It seemed, with these two men, that she could never hold on, and she thrust once, twice, once more before she gave over to the intensity, the cosmic pleasure, and came shuddering hard and aggressively around Sawyer's cock. Cade thrust just once more, then he was pumping into her ass and gripping her skin tight enough to leave marks. Hollie didn't want to think about the idea of being marked by him or how very much it appealed to her.

Distantly, she registered Sawyer giving over to his own pleasure and pumping hard as he thrust, before finally slumping back on the bed.

For a moment, the three of them remained still and quiet, enjoying the after-effects of their pleasure in this oasis, free from prying eyes. Sawyer removed the toy from her mouth and Cade released the bindings around her wrists, then the nipple clamps. Hollie gave her wrists an experimental twist and sighed at the relief of sensation.

Slowly, Cade pulled free from her body and Hollie began to climb off Sawyer until they were no longer one functioning machine of power and pleasure but three individuals who had a very challenging time of keeping their hands to themselves.

Cade came in a moment later with warm clothes and Hollie cleaned up then accepted the glass of water he handed her. It was, after all, one of the perks of being with a Dom—the sweet, quiet moments afterward where they wrapped her in a blanket and held her close.

Which he was doing now, taking the water from her hand and pulling her into his arms. She noticed that he left her in the middle of the bed, to allow Sawyer, who had just returned from the bathroom, to cuddle up on her other side.

"What do we do now?" she asked, because the silence was stretching and they had come down to talk and she knew that she was terrified she would get into that Jeep and drive back to Denver without once looking behind her. She, the consummate explorer, adventurer and traveler, the risk taker, the diver, climber and rescuer, was scared out of her mind.

Because what if they didn't ask her to stay, what if they didn't try to get her to trust them? What if this, whatever was really going on between them all right now, really was the end of the line?

"You have to tell us, Hollie," Sawyer said. He was looking at the ceiling and not at her, and Hollie knew things couldn't be any easier for them than they were for her.

Still, she knew what she wanted them to say, knew what she needed them to say to make everything real, everything possible.

She wanted them to ask her to stay.

She hadn't realized it in the beginning. Not up until the conversation with Dec, not until the moment they had worked so hard to give her so much pleasure. It hadn't been one moment. It had been every moment between them, everything real and delicious and lovely, everything hard and nostalgic and important. She wanted one of them, both of them, right now, right at this moment, to ask her to stay.

"I'm not going to choose between the two of you," she said. "I wasn't able to do it then and I'm certainly no more capable of doing it now." She took a deep sigh. Sleeping together was one thing, but the kind of relationships her friends shared with their partners was something else entirely, something they hadn't touched on. And hell, they hadn't touched on it for a very good reason. *But if not now, when?*

Take that leap of faith, Hollie…

"What about something else…"

The two men at her side stiffened, each in their own unique way. Every muscle in Sawyer's body went rigid, as if he were about to perform some feat of physical power and magnitude. Cade practically stopped breathing.

"You're talking about the kind of relationships Lily and Maddy have," Cade said quietly. Of course, it was the first time in all the years they had known each other where Hollie truly couldn't figure out the emotion behind his words, and that scared her all the more.

And yet, she was talking about those relationships because they worked, because she had never seen Dec or Micah so damn happy, because Lily and Maddy were perfectly comfortable, perfectly at ease and more than loved in their relationships, and Hollie didn't think it was too damn much to want something like it.

"They're happy," she pointed out, instead of answering the question. "They're all very much in love."

'Love is complicated,' Dec had said, but their love was no more complicated than anyone else's, and they were so very happy, so very together forever.

"What if it's too hard?" Sawyer asked quietly on her other side. "What if we can't make it work between us? We lose everything." 'Everything' being the relationship they could have shared, being the relationship they still could share if someone told her what was going on in their heads right now.

Ask me to stay.

She wasn't going to beg. She was going to take their leads. If they wanted her to stay, they would have asked for it.

She wanted to be worth asking for.

Before she got the chance to say anything, not that Hollie had any idea what the proper thing to say was in a circumstance like this, her phone started vibrating against the floor.

She was out of bed in a flash, ready for the worst news. When she saw Savannah's number on the screen, she knew it couldn't be good.

"The bridge is already flooded," Savannah said, in lieu of a greeting. "I'm going to need to get you and some guys down here. I can't get through to Sawyer and Cam is calling Cade right now." Sure enough, Cade's phone was buzzing on the table where he had left it. "I've got calls for them too."

"Where do they need to go?" Hollie asked, yanking on a fresh pair of underwear and her utilitarian socks and waterproof boots while she spoke. "I'll get them there."

Savannah rattled off the zones and Hollie nodded and asked her pressing questions, before she hung up.

"Cade, accident on second with minor injuries but line damage. I need to you to take point on that until the power is cut off. Sawyer, we've got two trees down near the road out of town and potential fire hazards in the surrounding area — that's over on Fifth and Main."

She chanced a look outside at the darkening sky with its ominous clouds and promises of surefire damage to come.

"The storm is here," she said. "We'll finish this conversation right after we're done keeping this town safe."

Chapter Fifteen

Cade dealt with the downed electricity pole in less than an hour, but the storm that had started as a slow drizzle while he had been leaving Hollie's cabin had turned into a full-on raging thunderstorm and he'd stopped for his fair share of accidents, people out of their homes and other emergencies. The wind was kicking up, and he was able to help pull some trees out of the line of danger and prevent a couple of disasters with the winch on his truck and good old-fashioned grit and vinegar.

He'd caught up with Cam at the intersection to downtown, where they were working on unclogging several of the sewage drains that had become backed up, to help reduce the overflow into the streets. But though they continued to work to clear the drainage systems and prevent buildup, the streets began to flood, water rising to the tops of the rainboots he had been glad Cam insisted he wear.

For a thousand reasons, he was grateful Hollie had been sent their way, to help prepare evacuation plans and ensure the town had options if the flood levels rose — as they were doing now. It was impossible to see much beyond his own face, but Cade knew the mountains would look different if he could see them, the white caps replaced with deep, steel gray, darker than the murky water at his feet and the sky open and angry above them.

And though his hands were freezing and his entire body was soaked — except for the toes of his socks because — *thanks, Cam* — those boots were doing wonders, Cade couldn't stop thinking about all the other reasons he was happy Hollie had come back. She had reminded him of who he was, given him the chance to see beyond his own memories, to understand the value of all that he had accomplished and how he might manage so much more.

And she wanted...

She wanted something Cade wasn't sure he could give. It wasn't even that he and Sawyer had been fighting for nearly a decade — though they had been fighting over her, which did make things more and less complicated at the same time. No, it wasn't even Sawyer. It was the whole idea of sharing the woman who he'd never stopped thinking about with someone else, of not being enough for her all on his own.

And yet, it wasn't that he wasn't enough. Cade understood that from watching how the Hollis sisters interacted with their partners. Lily and Maddy Hollis gave their full hearts to both men in their lives without question, as if each of their partners fulfilled some fundamental but different role.

Sawyer, though? Sawyer, who he'd been fighting with for years, a man he barely managed civility toward and the same in return?

Because you both love her. Because you've both always loved her.

Damn it, that was the truth of it, wasn't it? Sawyer Matthews would be the perfect person to have such an arrangement with because Sawyer was the only other man in the world who loved Hollie the way Cade did.

Which meant.

Which meant... *Fuck.*

"Cade!" It was impossible to hear anything over the sound of the storm and they worked to dam the flooding and prevent it from damaging the buildings and homes along the street front, but the expression on Cam's face had him moving to her as quickly as he could.

"Savannah can't get through to Hollie," she shouted over the storm, holding up her radio, which had been unceremoniously shoved into a Ziploc bag. "Wants to know if we're able to find her."

Cade nodded, but it felt as though his stomach was the runoff location for the storm, churning with muck and grime as he thought about where she might be and what might have happened so she wasn't able to respond.

Her radio's probably busted. It's no big deal.

But there was no denying the way his panic rose at the thought of something happening to her, and Cade made for higher ground with Cam quick on his heels. They took shelter under the awning of the nearest shop and he pulled his own radio free from his slicker.

It was static then buzzing and the weakest connection, and he fiddled with the dials for a moment.

"Sawyer, do you read?"

It was nearly impossible to hear, but Cade didn't care. It suddenly felt imperative that Sawyer was out there looking for Hollie alongside Cade and their years of arguing and fighting could be forgotten in a single afternoon.

"I'm here, Sheriff," Sawyer said, coming in rough, but there nonetheless.

"We can't find Hollie," he said. "Cam's going to meet up with Savannah. Rendezvous at Hollie's house and go from there?"

It was the first thing that had come to his mind, but he had to do *something*. Cam gave him a nod and headed to the cruiser she had parked at the top of the hill as Cade made his way to his truck. Hollie's house, the house he had practically grown up in, the house with the grandmother who had cared and the brother who had teased and the hot meals and the friendly smiles, was only a few miles down the road and he navigated around the raging rivers of water in the streets and toward the far side of the tracks. They'd all grown up on the wrong side of town, Hollie, Sawyer and him, and they'd all found their way up the ladder, becoming the best, most capable versions of themselves.

Almost.

Cade had a sneaking suspicion that the best version of himself involved Hollie Callihan in his life and, inexplicably and annoyingly, it involved Sawyer Matthews too.

Sawyer was already pulling down the street by the time Cade arrived and the damage to the small road was apparent at first sight. Two of the largest, oldest trees lay on their sides in the middle of the road and blocked both cars from getting any farther. Cade parked behind him and hopped out, meeting Sawyer's stride, and they headed for the back of the house, calling her name, trying to be heard over the sounds of the howling wind and beating rain.

They didn't need to say anything, not now, not with Hollie missing and the storm raging around them, but Sawyer wanted to. He wanted to say that he understood what Cade was telling him by sharing the call. For every tree they'd moved, every sandbag they had placed, he had thought of Hollie, of how she had voiced a willingness to try, but one that was all in, both or neither. She had been so bold and open, willing to lay herself out on the line – it put both him and Cade to shame.

What had truly come as a surprise, however, was that he wasn't immediately turned off by the idea. Oh, sure, there were other men in the world he'd rather hitch his horse to the same wagon with, but Cade had loved Hollie as long and as deeply as Sawyer himself had...

Am I completely fucking nuts to consider this?

He wasn't even sure what he was really considering. All Sawyer knew was that if Hollie left them again, that would undoubtedly be the end of him and his chance for love.

And if following love and forever and the fairytale bullshit that never came for guys like him meant thinking a little outside of the box, meant opening up his mind a little more than he had ever expected...

Sawyer was up for the adventure.

"She's not here," Cade said, looking around and pointing the flashlight he'd just pulled from his pocket at the various corners of the estate.

"Where was she when the call came?" Sawyer asked, then he and Cade were running back to the cars before they even finished the reply.

The bridge.

They didn't even discuss it. Cade just climbed into Sawyer's truck and Sawyer sent muddy wheels spinning when he pulled backward and hauled ass across town. Hollie had been called away to check on the flooded bridge, but that had been hours ago. Surely she was somewhere else by now. Surely nothing had happened to her.

But the idea that something *had* happened to her, that she might not be waiting for them with quips and clever remarks, that she might never share her sense of adventure with the world again, that any harm at all might have befallen her, made the rest of it disappear. Sawyer didn't have any anger left, not toward Hollie for having left them all those years ago, not even toward Cade, whom he'd blamed for so long and who wasn't any more responsible for her leaving than Sawyer himself. There was no anger left, just the hope that she was still okay and the willingness to do whatever it would take to ensure she stayed with them in the future.

Before Sawyer could give voice to any of that, however, they arrived at the bridge. Sort of. He couldn't pull up any closer than two dozen yards. The road leading to the bridge and the two riverbanks were submerged, as was the bridge itself. It was like something out of an apocalyptic film — raging, dirty waters coming hard down from the mountains, the crossing of the bridge gone below the surface and...

And Hollie hanging on to one beam with all her might. Sawyer's heart kicked into high gear and he parked and raced out of the car, stopping to grab a length of thick, solid rope from the trunk and coming to meet Cade when they ventured toward her.

"Hollie!" Cade called from beside him, but there was no way she could hear them, not with the raging water all around her and the powerful surge of rain still coming down.

"Here." Sawyer uncoiled the rope and attached one carabiner to the hook on Cade's jacket, then attached the other to his own. A third length of cord was wrapped around the middle of their ties and hooked to the front of the car, making a T shape and allowing them to both take that first step out into the muddy water. It was high and angry, the floods coming nearly up to his waist. They would have been so much higher on Hollie's petite frame, and he had to wonder how long she had been out there, holding on to the metal beam for her life — what she had been thinking about as she had held tight.

It's you, Hollie. It's always been you.

And if that meant taking a chance on the man beside him, Sawyer was willing to do it. He hadn't gotten along with Cade Easton for years — and not for the right reasons. But regardless, they had saved lives together and kept Wolf Creek safe and secure, all while griping and bitching about it. Imagine the kind of the good they could do for the town if they happily worked together...

To start, however, they had to work together on getting Hollie home safe. In fact, it was the only thing that mattered at all. *Hollie.* Hollie was the only thing that had ever truly mattered. And Sawyer was about to prove it.

The going was slow, against the rage of the current, but they were able to walk at the same pace half pushing against the water and pulling themselves along by the beams of the bridge, until they were five feet from Hollie, then three, then one.

She was soaking wet and her teeth were clearly chattering. Even as far away as they were, that was impossible to miss. She otherwise looked unharmed, though, and Sawyer sent up a prayer to whatever god was listening that they got her off the broken beam and home safe.

"Can you reach my hand?" he asked, holding on to one beam of the bridge while he stretched out his hand. It was nearly six inches too far away. Hollie reached, but she couldn't get to him, and Sawyer knew the other beam, laden down with water now, would never support both their weights. Even when she moved slightly toward him, the damn thing began to creak and sway, just like floorboards giving way during a fire. He'd take fire over water any day of the week.

"Just hold on," Cade shouted from Sawyer's side. "We're coming."

Sawyer wasn't exactly sure how, but then Cade was scaling the side of the bridge and trying to come down to grab Hollie's hand from above. The water below her was getting higher and the beam she was on was rocking violently now. Cade got her hand. Sawyer could see the moment their grips met—the same moment the beam snapped in half and they fell into the roiling water.

For a moment, he couldn't see either of them and Sawyer thought that he had officially lost everything, but then a head of blonde hair, then brown popped up a few feet down—*damn, that river's really moving*—and Sawyer felt the tug on the rope around his waist.

Thank god.

It was slow going pulling them both to safety, but he'd spent his years as a firefighter hauling heavier loads. It wouldn't have mattered if the two of them hanging on to the rope had weighed as much as his truck, Sawyer would have put one hand over the other until they were safely back on their feet. The waters were rising and he did his best to keep his movements steady and even, to prevent his arms from tiring, and eventually Cade was able to place his feet on something and the rope eased when he and Hollie, half holding on to him and half supporting him, were able to reach the bridge.

Or what was left of it. The water was now at the second rung of the metal support beams and surging higher, and everything Sawyer had dismissed as the fear mongering bureaucrats overreacting to nature's expected chaos had come to pass. Their little town was underwater—and they had done their best to save it from the worst of things.

Hollie half-swam and half-walked across the bridge, Cade right behind her. The water was up past his elbow, and on Hollie that meant higher than her shoulder, and rising steadily. She reached out and he grabbed her hand and with the other one she reached for Cade. Then, without words, the three of them began their slow, steady march across the flooded bridge to higher banks. Together.

Chapter Sixteen

Hollie had climbed pyramids, mountains and towers. She had set up camp on the edge of a volcano. Once, while scuba diving in South America, her partner's tank had failed, and the two of them had made the world's slowest ascent, sharing air while moving toward the surface.

None of it, not the hiking or rock climbing, had tired her bones and worn her muscles the way clinging to the edge of that bridge for nearly an hour had done. She let go of both Cade and Sawyer's hands and half-sat, half-fell onto the muddy banks at the edge of the river. Her legs were aching like all hell, but it was her arms that burned and she knew it would be some time before she was able to so much as run a comb through her hair.

But it didn't matter. They had saved her. They had realized she was missing and they had come out to find her. She didn't want to think about how much longer she would have been able to cling to that broken beam. All she wanted at the moment was a warm bed and something strong to drink.

"We found her." Cade's voice was difficult to hear over the sound of the rain beating around them, but she glanced up to see him holding the walkie talkie close to his mouth. "Bridge is flooded, but the dam seems to be holding on the downstream. We're coming back to you."

It must have been Cam or Savannah he was talking to, and despite her exhaustion, her duty pushed her to her feet.

"How's the rest of the town?" she asked, steadying herself against the side of Sawyer's truck when the dizziness caught her by surprise.

"Sandbags are holding," Sawyer said, his voice gruff and his expression dark. "We have downed trees on Main and off the Route Two ramp, but so far no residential dangers."

Hollie closed her eyes and took a deep breath. Then another. There was no way this flood wasn't going to wreak havoc on the town, but they had done their best to ensure that everyone and almost everything was as safe as possible.

"Are you okay?" Cade asked, and his voice was too sympathetic, too concerned for her liking. She was in control, damn it. She would have found a way out of this bind just as she had every other bind she had ever been in.

But the floods raged around them and Hollie knew that there had been a chance she wouldn't have made it out alive without their coming for her, and she finally opened her eyes.

"I am now," she said quietly, too quietly, as if the strength that had kept her from letting go was all gone now and it was a wonder she was even still standing.

"Good." With that, Cade picked her up in a single, swift movement and carried her to the back seat of Sawyer's truck. He didn't bother to put her down, simply climbed in with her on his lap and held close. Hollie hadn't realized how desperately she needed to be held close until this very moment.

Without another word, Sawyer climbed into the front seat and pulled the truck away from the raging riverbank. They made their way back toward the Triple Diamond Ranch and Hollie's eyes sagged closed. It felt like only a moment had passed, but when Cade gently woke her, they had arrived. The tent she had set up earlier in the week had been taken down and the ground was muddy and streaked with steady streams of water, but through the shade of intense sheets of rain, Hollie couldn't make out any structural damage to the homes or cabins.

She was carried gently but quickly into the lodge, and when they entered, she felt the weight of a dozen pairs of eyes on her.

"Oh, thank God." That was Savannah, who was pulling her first aid kid from the table and bringing it over to the couch when Hollie demanded Cade finally put her down. Maddy and Lily Hollis were there, as well as Dec and Micah, Ryder and Christian and Camilla. Around the room, she spied a few piles of wet towels and one or two buckets catching the stray drops.

Savannah fussed over her, poking and prodding, and sending Sawyer and Cade half scampering away in fear. *Trust the redhead farm girl to do what a natural disaster couldn't.*

"You scared the fucking daylights out of me," Savannah said. She shined a flashlight into Hollie's eyes and directed her to look up, then down, then side to side. Apparently satisfied, she wrapped the blood pressure gauge around Hollie's arm and continued in below-the-breath mutters and swear words. She peeled open a chocolate bar and practically forced a few bites into Hollie's mouth.

"You're not just my boss, Hollie Callihan. You're a goddamn inspiration..." She glanced up and caught Hollie's eyes, and Hollie could actually see a sheen of tears. "You're my friend. I know you don't like to hear that. I know you don't like to settle or have too many roots in one place, but there it is. You're my friend and I don't want anything to happen to you, damnit."

Hollie almost knocked Savannah off the couch when she wrapped her in a hug.

"You're my friend too, Sav," she managed, the words catching in her throat. Across the room, she spied Cade and Sawyer in deep conversation, one that, for the first time since she'd arrived, didn't appear fraught with tension. "And I think I might be okay with putting a few roots down."

Savannah turned and followed her gaze, then gave her a dazzling smile.

"Then I'm happy for you," she said quietly. "I'll give you guys a minute."

She grabbed her bag of equipment and beat a hasty retreat to the card room near the door, where apparently everyone else had gathered to provide their trio a little bit of privacy. There was something to be said about her love life being so obvious. At least there wasn't any beating around the bush.

"Are you okay?" It was Sawyer who asked this time, and in the bright, clear room, she could see the depths of his worry in those dark green eyes.

Hollie nodded. "I am." She held up the chocolate bar in her hand. "Chocolate cures all problems."

Before she could even finish, Sawyer pushed her back against the couch and kissed her roughly and possessively, claiming her mouth with a fierceness that rivaled the storm outside. She kissed back, her body responding to his touch with a wildness that only came from surviving something insane, with a need she barely knew from inside herself.

Eventually, they were able to pull apart and Hollie instinctively glanced at Cade. To her surprise, he wore only an expression of mind amusement, laced with something darker and more promising.

"We should have given you an answer before we left," Cade said quietly. He settled on the table before the couch and looked her directly in the eye. "I was scared. Hell, Hol, we were both scared. It's a lot to ask."

She went to respond but he cut her off with a shake of the head, and she let him continue.

"It's a lot to ask, but it doesn't matter. When we saw you out on the bridge, Hollie, my heart jumped out of my fucking chest and I realized it doesn't matter how I get to have you in my life or who I get to love you alongside, only that I do. Whatever you need, I'm willing to do it because I love you, Hollie Callihan. Completely."

Hollie's heart felt huge in her chest and she turned to Sawyer, who was sitting on the couch next to her, idly stroking the back of her neck with his strong, capable hands.

"Cade's the poet," he said, and she didn't miss the use of Cade's first name. "But me too, Hollie. I fucking love you. And I know he does too."

She closed her eyes, hearing the words but not quite able to make sense of them, hoping mingling with fear, mingling with excitement.

"What are you guys saying?" she asked, desperate evident in her voice. If they meant...

"Be ours, Hollie," Cade said plainly. "Both of ours. We can't promise it'll be easy or that we'll suddenly become best friends, but we're willing to do whatever it takes to be with you."

She burst into tears. She didn't mean to. She wasn't a crier by nature, but the events of the day, with the flooding and the nearly dying and the hurt she had felt walking away from them and now the overwhelming joy that bubbled to the surface and pushed everything else along with it, had her overflowing like a fountain.

Sawyer's hand stilled on her neck and Hollie let out a laugh that sounded more like a hiccup. Leave it to two of the most capable, heroic men she'd ever met to act like deer in the headlights at the sight of a woman crying. Well, she'd change that — now that she had the chance.

"Happy tears," she managed. "So happy."

Wet from the river and rain and her own joy, Hollie leaned forward and kissed Cade squarely on the mouth. Then she turned and did the same to Sawyer.

"I love you both," she managed, through her overwhelming emotion. "I always have. I was just too scared to admit it until now." She paused and met both of their gazes. "Thank you for giving me the chance to realize the best thing in my life."

The two of them embraced her and she welcomed the capable, protective hold around her. She wasn't sure how long she stayed like that, only that the sound of Savannah sighing deeply and Camilla uttering a *finally,* brought her back to the room around her and their group of friends now gathering at the couch.

"Were you guys spying?" Hollie asked. Dec's face was way too innocent and Micah just raised an eyebrow.

"You think we're going to let two of Wolf Creek's most notorious hardasses admit their undying love without watching?" Cam asked, her own voice so neutral and bland that Hollie couldn't help but let out a watery laugh.

"We tried to stop them," Christian added unhelpfully, but one glowering look from Maddy gave Hollie all the insight she needed into how much Christian Harlow and Ryder Dean—two more of the town's bad boys lost to love—had been ear-to-the-door for their supposedly private scene.

"I think this calls for a toast," Lily said. She slid over to the other side of the bar and popped open a bottle of champagne. She poured the flutes quickly and passed them around, then raised one of her own.

"To love in the storm," she said.

The group of them echoed with their own toasts, and Hollie raised her glass, looked first to Sawyer, then to Cade. They'd been wading through their deep waters for so long, and now the skies had finally cleared, bringing sunshine to the love that had long existed between them.

Love in the storm, indeed.

Epilogue

"And when you anticipate northern flooding, the best course of action is to stem the dam from the northeast corridor, like we did in this example," Hollie explained, indicating a large map projected against the screen. The small group of people in the room were nodding along and taking notes, and Hollie moved to switch to the next slide when she saw Dec standing in the corner.

"It's lunch time," he said, glancing to the clock on the far side of the room. "I thought Micah was the hardass professor, but you have to let them eat, Hol."

Hollie smiled and nodded and the small group of search and rescue and emergency responder experts who were attending Micah and Dec's training camp — her training camp — began gathering their belongings to head down to the mess hall on the far side of the grounds. But Dec didn't leave right away. Instead, he walked farther into the room and waited until all their students had departed to lean against the side of the desk and cross his arms with a knowing smile.

"You've got some guests, professor," he said, and Hollie had to resist the urge to smack the smug smile off his face. In the months since Dec and Micah had offered her a position teaching with their survival program, she'd grown closer to both of them and to Lily, and allowed her roots to flourish and settle. They had Sunday dinners at the Triple Diamond Ranch and Hollie had planted a garden, a *garden*, literal proof of her roots, as she found her own version of home in the small town where she had grown up, the town she had been so desperate to leave.

But it was the presence of the two men who shared her bed and her life that would have made Wolf Creek the place she wanted to rest her head, even if Savannah hadn't followed her back to join to Wolf Creek Police Force, even if Maddy and Lily hadn't welcomed her into the family with open arms, even if their friend Ev hadn't arranged for Federal Agent Emergency Training Programs at the Wolf Creek Survival Camp, taught specifically by Hollie.

It was the way the sun shone through the back window to her little house early in the morning, when Sawyer cooked pancakes and Cade growled at the coffeemaker. It was the way the two of them, in companionable silence, had worked together to add a large extension on the back of the home, as they'd collected first a stray cat, then a litter of puppies, then, inexplicably, a goat, who had wandered onto the property one day and simply never left. It was the way they had both sacrificed so very much to be with her, for the opportunity to love her, and had never once mentioned it again.

It was falling asleep, sated and safe, and waking up in the arms of the men she loved.

"Where are they?" she asked Dec, who, damn him, definitely knew something she didn't know.

"Out on the ridge," he said, "It's cooler out there."

Summer was on the rise in Wolf Creek and she had gathered with the Hollis sisters on more than one occasion to marvel at how all their lives had changed so incredibly in merely a year, from the day Maddy had inherited her uncle's ranch, to Lily's visiting for her graduate program, to the wedding where their friend Ev had found that love had been right in front of her the entire time, to the return Hollie had made to a town she had never thought she would visit again. A year, and all four of them were more in love than they had been on day one, no matter how unorthodox or different each relationship was.

Hollie moved to the door and absently patted the front pocket of her light spring jacket. Two small boxes nestled in the lining and out of sight. She'd been feeling that pocket for the better part of a month, waiting for the perfect opportunity.

Dec called her name and Hollie turned around to see his face break into a grin.

"Go easy on 'em, Hol," he said.

Furrowing her brow and trying not to smile, Hollie left the small lodge and headed down to the ridge. It was a sprawling, beautiful vignette. The Black Reef Mountains were awash in every shade of green around, above and below them, and pockets of wild flowers dotted the mountain's edge. Truly, Wolf Creek had become nothing short of a paradise for her.

At the sight of Cade and Sawyer standing in a small cleaning, Hollie's heart felt lighter and fuller all at the same time. They had their share of challenges — every relationship did. But they had survived the storm together, quite literally, and had been a team ever since. Cade and Sawyer's friendship was unique, deeper for their having been at odds for so long. But whether the men admitted it aloud or not, they loved each other as fiercely as brothers and were both better people for the closeness they shared.

"What's all this?" Hollie asked, indicating to the small picnic blanket set with plates and bowls and a large pitcher of tea on a tray. "You guys are spoiling me."

"Every day," Cade said, pulling her to his side and holding her possessively against him. Sawyer flashed her a grin.

"Every day for the rest of our lives," he said. The two men glanced at each other with friendly, knowing smiles she would have thought impossible three months before. Then, as if they had practiced it in unison, both sank to their knees before her.

"Hollyhock." It was Cade who spoke first, and if she wasn't imagining it, his eyes were definitely shiny. "We don't want to leave anything up to fate, or chance or natural disaster." He pulled a small ring box from his pocket and held it before her.

Sawyer did the same and continued, "It hasn't been very long since you returned to Wolf Creek, but we know how we feel about you and we want the whole world to know too." They both opened their boxes and Hollie gasped at the simple, elegant designs each of them displayed.

"Will you handfast with us?" Cade asked. "Both of us?"

"Forever?" Sawyer added.

God, it was something heady to have two beautiful men down on their knees before her.

"On one condition," Hollie said, trying and failing to contain her grin. Twin eyebrows rose in response.

"You will both handfast with me." She pulled the two boxes from her own pocket and handed the deep blue velvet one to Cade and the deep red velvet one to Sawyer. She had picked rings that matched each man, Sawyer's bold and gentle at the same time, done in a style of carbon fiber and wood. Cade's was subtle and intricate, a printed pattern designed in sterling silver, and a wild possessive feeling settled over Hollie as she helped both men slide the rings she had chosen for them onto their strong, capable fingers.

And by the time all three boxes were open, Hollie, Cade and Sawyer were misty-eyed and quiet in the beauty of the moment. Hollie realized they had chosen a set of interlocking rings, ones that connected together with two gemstones and sleek rose-gold bands. They fitted perfectly into one another and perfectly on her finger.

"So that's a yes then," Cade asked, coming to stand at her side.

Hollie simply kissed him. Then she turned and kissed Sawyer, and she very well might have taken them both down to the picnic blanket if Dec's wolf whistle hadn't had her turning around to see her their friends and family pouring from the lodge, where they'd undoubtedly been watching the entire scene.

She raised one eyebrow at the two men, but Sawyer just shrugged. "It's love," he said. "People love love in all forms." He pinched her ass and Hollie got the distinct impression it was because he felt he needed to retain some of his masculine facade. "Plus, they got a great show…" She grinned and allowed herself to be absorbed by the group of their friends and family, taking the hugs from Savannah and Lily and Maddy and Wes...

Wes.

"Surprised?" he asked, pulling her into a hug. "I got in about fifteen minutes ago, so good timing."

She squeezed her brother tightly and looked up to meet blue eyes so similar to her own.

"I thought you were in South America," she said, not even bothering to hide the tears of joy that were fully streaming down her face now.

"I was," he said. "And I'll go back soon. But the way I see it, you're my home, Hollie, and it's time I come back for a bit."

She wrapped her arms around him, around their friends and, eventually, around the men she dearly loved. For this day, as they celebrated love in its many forms, friendship, family affection, romance, for the night, as they lost each other in the deep throes of pleasure, and for decades to come, Cade and Sawyer remained Hollie's safe ports, and she worked every day to be theirs. Their story was proof that family could be found if a woman only knew where to look and that, with love and good people by her side, she could truly weather any storm — as long as they were together.

Want to see more like this?
Here's a taster for you to enjoy!

Red Wolves Motorcycle Club: Along Came Merrie
Beth D. Carter

Excerpt

Merrie eased up on the gas when she finally accepted the truth. She was lost. Miles from nowhere, she looked down at her gas tank light flickering dangerously low. She dug around on the passenger seat until she found her phone then illuminated it to check her bars.

Of course. Dead.

Story of her life—dead end jobs, dead end future. She'd been taking care of herself since before she should've and the only job she'd been able to get at age fifteen was working on a dairy farm. It was nice but it didn't pay all that much, and she'd gotten tired of her ass being grabbed each time she came by with the coffee carafe. The idea of moving to Cheyenne had sounded good at the time but now—lost in the middle of Wyoming—somehow it didn't seem all that smart. Why was it that none of the roads had marker signs?

She'd gotten turned around at that last pit stop— that's what had happened. Too many roads branched out for the truckers and she'd become confused about which road she'd been on. She was always doing stupid things like that. How hard was it to follow a road?

Apparently, very hard.

It only added to the melancholy lingering in her soul. She had wanted to start over, begin a new chapter in her life, so she'd donated most of her stuff to charity, keeping only the items that were important. It had depressed the hell out of her when she'd discovered all her worldly possessions had fitted in her trunk. It wasn't as if she'd had a happy childhood full of memorabilia and crap. Hell, she'd barely graduated high school.

A glow in the distant sky lifted her spirits. A glow meant people, civilization. Hopefully it also meant a gas station or maybe someone who had information on how far the next one was — and food would be a plus. She hadn't eaten since the truck stop a few hours ago.

She pressed harder on the gas pedal. The quicker she reached the lights, the quicker she'd get back on the right track. Merrie kept her fingers crossed that she wasn't too far from her destination. Who knew driving could be so exhausting?

Her focus stayed on the lights and, as she grew closer, the shape of a large barn converted into a bar drew closer. Dozens of motorcycles surrounded it, big silver and black monstrosities that pushed a slither of unease down her spine. The only bikers she'd really heard of were the made up ones on television and they were dangerous bad asses. Plus, being a woman had her naturally distrustful of bars. There were too many horror stories where a girl went into a bar never to be seen again, and this one held bikers. She slowed upon noticing an old public telephone booth toward the back of the building. Never mind that it belonged in a museum — relief poured through her. She wouldn't have to go inside to ask for directions. She could simply call the police to help her.

Merrie flicked off her headlights as she pulled into the parking lot then headed around back near the telephone booth. She didn't see anyone, so she turned off her car and opened the door. Getting out, she looked around and took a step toward the call box when she heard a man laugh. She swung around. In the shadows of the building, two men talked and shook hands. They wore leather vests with many patches on them but one of the men had a band of red running along the bottom of his while the other didn't. The second man faced her, the patch on his vest white with a red devil and two Ds on it.

Suddenly, the bearded man who faced her turned his head and looked directly at her. He tapped the other guy on the shoulder and he spun on his heel too. The second biker, his goatee cut close to his chin, glared at her like she was something disgusting on the bottom of his shoe. Seriously creeped out, Merrie debated if she should get back in her car and just leave. The telephone stood only a few feet away. Without knowing where she was, she had no way to judge how far the next gas stop would be. Did she really want to be stuck out in the middle of nowhere? Mind made up, she pushed her misgivings away as she hurried over to the phone.

She picked up the receiver, heard a dial tone and breathed a sigh of relief. It worked! She dug in her jeans pocket for some coins and was just about to put them into the phone, when a hand twisted in her hair and pulled sharply. Needle-like pain pricked her scalp and Merrie raised her hands instinctively, trying to alleviate the throb. The phone receiver fell to dangle at the bottom of the phone box.

"Ouch!"

The man holding her hair jerked her away from the phone booth. He twisted his hand, bringing her head up so she stared into his face. Tears flooded her eyes.

"Who are you?" he demanded.

"Let go of me!" she yelled, trying to free herself. This wasn't the first time she'd dealt with this type of torment. Her mother had liked to hurt her whenever she was in her drunken rages.

The biker backhanded her. White-hot heat exploded in her cheek as the force of the hit spun her around. Dirt filled her mouth as she landed hard on her front and tears filled her eyes when her nerve endings processed the pain. Fear replaced every single coherent thought and instinct in Merrie's mind. She pushed herself up and glanced at the man, holding her hands out in a pleading gesture for him to leave her alone.

"I asked who you are," he said coldly. "I didn't ask for a fucking attitude."

"M-my name is M-Merrie," she whimpered, spitting out dirt and blood. Her teeth had cut the inside of her mouth. "P-please don't hurt me."

"Merrie. Well, Merrie, who were you calling?"

"N-no one," she said.

He grabbed her arm and yanked her up to stand in front of him. He bent her arm behind her until she whimpered and tried to pull away, but his grip was too tight.

"Now why don't I believe you?" He shook her. "Were you calling the club? Are you someone's old lady? Or just a fucking spy?"

"I don't know any club. Please let me go!"

"Who were you calling?" he demanded again. This time he brought his hand back in a fist.

"The police!" she cried, cringing.

He leered in her face. The stale stench of cigarettes and the sour fermentation of beer on his breath activated her gag reflex. But she swallowed down the bile. "I've got the police in my back pocket, you stupid bitch. They can't help you."

"I'm lost," she whispered, closing her eyes. "I swear. I was just calling them because I'm lost!"

"Well, shit," someone else said.

Merrie cracked her eyes open. The other man with the gray beard looked at her with a mixture of pity and resolution. Her heart pounded as fear skyrocketed to terror and she knew her life was in jeopardy. Once again, she tugged her arm, trying to break the tight grip on her wrist.

"You fucked up, Axe," the bearded man said. "And I don't know if she'd have someone come looking for her."

"I'll take care of it," Axe snarled.

"Make sure no one finds her body."

"No!" Merrie screamed. "I won't tell anyone anything. I swear. I-I've never been here. I don't even know where I am. Please don't hurt me. Please!"

"Shut up," Axe snarled. He drew back his fist again and smashed it into her face.

Her vision faded and she gave in to the beckoning darkness.

Home of Erotic Romance

Sign up for our newsletter and find out about all our romance book releases, eBook sales and promotions, sneak peeks and FREE romance books!

About the Author

Gemma Snow loves high heat, high adventures and high expectations for her heroes! Her stories are set in the past and present, from the glittering streets of Paris to cowboy-rich Triple Diamond Ranch in Wolf Creek, Montana.

In her free time, she loves to travel, and spent several months living in a fourteenth-century castle in the Netherlands. When not exploring the world, she likes dreaming up stories, eating spicy food, driving fast cars and talking to strangers. She recently moved to Nashville with a cute redheaded cat and a cute redheaded boy.

Gemma loves to hear from readers. You can find herr contact information, website details and author profile page at https://www.totallybound.com